The Widow
and the Wildcatter

Fran Baker

D0166974

DELPHI BOOKS

ISBN 0-9663397-8-9

Published in large print in 2005 by Delphi Books.

The text of this Large Print edition is unabridged. Other aspects of the book may vary from the original edition.

Set in 16 pt. Plantin by Steve Brooker

Printed in the United States on permanent paper.

Library of Congress Cataloging-in-Publication Data

Baker, Fran, 1947-
   The widow and the wildcatter / by Fran Baker.
      p. cm.
   ISBN-10: 0-9663397-8-9 (trade pbk. : alk. paper)
   ISBN-13: 978-0-9663397-8-9
1. Widows—Fiction. 2. Women farmers—Fiction.
3. Petroleum—Prospecting—Fiction. 4. Large type books.
I. Title.
   PS3552.A4265W53 2005
   813'.54—dc22
                                2005000309

Books by Fran Baker

Poetic Justice

Once A Warrior

The Lady and the Champ

San Antonio Rose

King of the Mountain

The Widow and the Wildcatter

Seeing Stars

On Love's Own Terms

Love in the China Sea

When Last We Loved

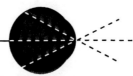

**This Large Print Book carries the
Seal of Approval of N.A.V.H.**

Prologue

The oil witch stood motionless in the corn-field, waiting for the spirit to move him.

His face, eyes closed, was turned to the endless sky. The wind threatened to blow his battered felt hat into the next county, but his arms remained glued to his sides, the palms of his hands parallel with the ground.

For his five-year-old daughter, watching from the edge of the field with her new-found friends, this was an everyday occurrence. The way Pa kept food in her belly and a little jingle in his pocket. But for the hardscrabble farmer and his pregnant wife, this was a last-ditch effort to change their luck.

The warm day gradually grew chilly as a wall of dirt—black mostly, but purple and tan and ocher too—advanced across the plains. Spindly redbuds and sturdy cotton-woods alike bowed to the will of the wind. A jackrabbit, light in the front legs but strong in the rear, took a far hill in a few bounds. Heading for a promised land of sunshine and oranges, like thousands of other Okies.

Suddenly the oil witch began to move.

His entire frame swayed to some intrinsic rhythm. Then round and round he turned in an ever-widening spiral, mumbling some kind of chant under his breath. At times his prancing became violent as he hovered over a certain spot, and then it subsided as he continued to spin.

Grit filled his eyes and mouth. Birds flew wildly over the field, some falling dead in midflight when dust clogged their lungs. Static electricity played over the farmer's old tin lizzie. No one even noticed.

At long last the oil witch stopped dancing and started shaking. His feet seemed stuck to one particular spot. Three, maybe four minutes passed while he stood there with sweat running down his face and the farmer and his wife both hoping and praying for the best.

He leaned forward then and lowered his palms toward the ground, moving them in a half circle as if he were groping for something in the dark. The upstart wind snatched his hat and sent it sailing. Spasms racked his body, growing more and more frenzied until he collapsed all in a heap.

The farmer thought surely the oil witch was dead.

His wife pulled a stub of a pencil from her

apron pocket and made a crude map on the back of a recipe for buttermilk pie.

The little girl broke a branch off a nearby bush and stuck it into the ground at her father's feet, then turned to the anxious young couple and announced, "There's your oil."

Chapter 1

"Mr. McCoy?"

"Up here!"

Joni looked up and saw the wildcatter frowning down at her from a narrow scaffold that had just been hoisted high above the rig floor.

"You don't know me," she yelled, "but—"

He crooked a hand to his ear and shook his head to indicate that he couldn't hear over the incessant din of men and machinery.

Dizziness assailed her as she considered her other option, and a sudden gust of wind intensified her dread. Then she remembered her reason for coming and, cupping both hands to her mouth like a megaphone, shouted at the top of her lungs. "How do I get up there?"

"You don't!" he hollered down, and emphasized his edict with a dismissive jerk of his thumb.

Joni realized he'd just ordered one of the half-dozen roughnecks working on the rig to "get rid of her," but she'd come too far to back down now.

Her fear of heights notwithstanding she marched toward a second scaffold that held a couple of lengths of pipe, one of which had a fishtail-shaped tool attached to the end of it.

"Sorry, ma'am." A rawboned man with a drawl as thick as January molasses grabbed her by the elbow before she could hop aboard. "The rig is off limits to outsiders."

"But—"

"No exceptions, ma'am."

Joni watched, secretly relieved as the scaffold started skyward without her. Top gun she wasn't. But neither was she giving up without a fight.

"You don't understand." She tried to reason with the roughneck first. "I've got to talk to Mr. McCoy. Today!"

Her escort kept a firm grip on her elbow as he steered her toward a long flight of steps that led to ground level. "Call him from home and leave a message on his answering machine."

"I've left messages—at least a dozen in the last two weeks alone," she argued to no avail. "He's never called me back."

"Mr. McCoy is a busy man." The roughneck didn't say "as any fool can see," but the sentiment was plastered all over his mud-spattered face. "Besides"—he skimmed her slender figure from the corner of his eye without breaking stride—"he's not much for mixing business with pleasure."

"But that's exactly what I've been trying to tell you!" At the bottom of the steps Joni stopped abruptly and pulled free of his hold. "This is business."

The man skidded to a halt and pushed his hard hat back off his forehead, revealing a receding hairline. "Well now, that's a horse of a different color."

"I should hope so!" she said.

His expression turned thoughtful. "In that case, leave the message with me and I'll give it to him when we're finished changing the drill bit."

"No."

"Why not?"

"It's too personal," she admitted reluctantly.

He looked at her as if she'd gone soft in the head. "Lady, make up your mind!"

Flushing, she said tensely, "It's business of a personal nature."

"Hey, Tex!" One of the workers on the rig captured his attention before he could form a reply. "Can you give me a hand with the draw works?"

"Be right there!" he assured the other rough-neck, eyeing his excess baggage uncertainly.

Joni saw her opportunity and seized it. "I'll wait here...cross my heart."

He threw his gloved hands into the air as if to say "Women!" Then, muttering an impatient curse under his breath, he turned and clomped back up the steps. At the top he stopped and tossed her one of the hard hats he'd plucked from a stack on the rig floor, shouting, "If you're gonna wait there, you've gotta wear this."

She caught the hard hat, put it on over her ponytail, and snapped him a crisp salute. "Thanks, Tex."

He shook his head and turned away, but not before she saw the ghost of a grin cross his lips.

Joni did as she'd promised and stayed put. While she waited for the wildcatter to change the bit and come back to earth, she compared this drilling site with the others she'd visited of late.

With very few exceptions, they all looked the same. An office trailer sat across the way, with a number of dirty pickup trucks—hers included—parked in front of it. Sunshine glanced off stacks of pipe that somehow resembled a great organ. The rig reached for the heavens, and thick red mud coated everything, even...

"My best jeans," she groused when she noticed the sticky substance clinging to her denim-covered legs with the tenacity of glue. Giving silent thanks that she'd decided to wear her waffle stompers instead of her tennis shoes, she craned her neck for a better view of the action.

Two more workers stood on the scaffold now, but Joni readily identified the wildcatter as the one in the middle. Like the rest of his crew he was dressed in steel-toed boots, mud-caked jeans, and a T-shirt that might have been white at one time. But there the resemblance ended.

Lithe and sinewy as a panther, he moved with the confidence of a man totally at ease with himself and with leading other men. And while he wore his hard hat tilted at a rakish angle, it was obvious to even the most casual observer that he ran a tight ship.

He stepped to the edge of the scaffold and picked up one of the pipes that Tex had helped hoist up to him. All eyes were riveted on his commanding figure, testifying to both the importance of what he was doing and the danger involved. Watching his men watch him with such open admiration, Joni could see why he was considered one of the best in the business.

The wind seemed to have hands as it shook the rig so relentlessly, and Joni's stomach crawled into her throat when she realized that the wildcatter was the only one up there who wasn't wearing a safety line. She wanted to look away but found she couldn't. It was as if she were hypnotized by the sheer horror of it.

He leaned out over the scaffold and began lowering the drill bit toward the square hole in the rig floor. Her fear for him mounted by leaps and bounds when the roughneck to his right fit a second pipe atop the first one, causing them to swing like an elongated pendulum. And when the third man reached out with a blowtorch to weld them together, she decided she'd seen enough and closed her eyes.

"Let 'er rip!" someone ordered a small eternity later.

Joni jumped when the diesel engine that powered the drill bit roared to life, and her eyes opened wide watching the scaffold safely return the three men to the rig floor.

When the wildcatter stepped off the plank, his crew closed ranks around him, laughing and slapping his back with beer-commercial heartiness.

The mud pump throbbed; steel clashed

13

on steel; and all was right with the rig again.

Standing off to the side, Joni felt totally excluded until Tex caught sight of her and pointed her out.

The wildcatter's jaw went hard as granite when he glanced her way, as if he saw something not to his liking.

As indeed he did.

Having just spent half the night and most of the morning on tour, the last thing he wanted to look at was some skinny female decked out like one of the boys. In fact, all he really wanted right now was a hot shower, a cold beer, and eight straight hours of shut-eye.

Joni kept her small face passive, though her skin paled under the country-girl freckles that were sprinkled across her nose and cheeks. Granted, she wouldn't win any beauty contests in this getup, but he wasn't exactly dressed to the nines himself.

She stood her ground, planning her approach.

He scowled down at her, plotting his escape.

She tipped her chin defiantly, and he found himself admiring the way she returned a man's direct gaze.

Their eyes remained locked as he sauntered

down the steps, but she was keenly conscious of the raw power concealed behind his loose-limbed stride. He pointed in the direction of the office trailer and, without a backward glance, headed that way.

Following suit, she was so tickled to think she'd finally found him that it was all she could do not to kick up her heels. But this was business, pure and simple, and recalling Tex's statement as he escorted her off the rig helped her to keep things in their proper perspective.

The wildcatter sloshed heedlessly through the mud puddle that had formed directly beneath the narrow metal step that led up to the trailer door, but Joni hesitated, hating to get her jeans any dirtier than they already were.

Unfortunately, she either had to go through the mud or jump over it. Judging the puddle to be about the length of a yardstick, she put her left foot forward, reared back on her right, and jumped.

She made it, but the step was slippery as oil and there was nothing for her to grab hold of. Nothing but...

At the same time the wildcatter extended a helping hand, Joni got a death grip on the front of his T-shirt. His patronizing grin drooped into a pained grimace when she seized a fistful of his chest hair in the process.

"Hey, lady, let go!"

"I'm afraid I'll fall!"

The fingers encircling her upper arm tightened, but the fierce expression on his face warned her she was pushing her luck. As did his ominously soft tone. "Let...go."

Joni got his message loud and clear. Either she let go or he did. She relaxed her grip and tried to collect her scattered wits while he rubbed that rock-solid chest with his free hand.

"Are you all right?" he asked. When he wasn't yelling, his voice was deep and just a shade raspy.

"Yes." She looked everywhere but into those eyes of April green, feeling like a big fool. "Thank you."

He released her arm. "So what do you want?"

She blinked, taken aback by his blunt demand. "I want to talk to you."

"I'm all ears," he said. But his muscular body said he was all man, and the step suddenly seemed half again as narrow as it had only moments before.

Swallowing nervously, she reached for the doorknob. But strong brown fingers beat her to the draw. She nodded her thanks and preceded him into the trailer, preparing to beard the lion in his den. Boar's nest would have been a better description.

Joni came to a halt not three feet beyond the threshold and stared around her in disbelief. In all her born days she'd never seen such disorder.

Blobs of red mud had been tracked across the linoleum floor and left to dry. Empty beer bottles and ashtrays filled to overflowing littered every available surface. A pinup girl wearing nothing but an Indian-style headband and a smile decorated an out-of-date wall calendar. The top of the desk looked fairly neat, but the sunlight that trickled in through the dusty blinds illuminated several nicks and one deep cigarette burn.

The wildcatter closed the door, shutting out most of the drilling noise, then pulled off his hard hat and hooked it on a wall peg. Combing his fingers through hair as black as Oklahoma crude, he crossed to the mini refrigerator in the corner and took out a beer.

"Beer for breakfast?" she asked, resenting his silence.

He turned to her then, his gaze raking over her with insulting thoroughness. "You got something better to offer?"

Joni was a little slow on the uptake, but when his words finally did sink in, her jaw dropped open in fury.

She yanked off her hard hat, aiming to give him a piece of her mind. The metal brim hit her ponytail holder, knocking it out of her hair and onto the floor. She turned to hang up her hat, thinking things couldn't get any worse, and found out how wrong she was when she accidentally kicked the barrette under the junk heap of a sofa that sat just a few feet away.

Her hair raining down her back like flames, she knelt beside the sofa and began rooting around underneath it.

"Get a move on, lady." The wildcatter's caustic tone made it clear that he had better things to do than to watch her imitate a demented anteater. "I happen to be busy."

"So I've heard," she muttered facetiously as she reached a mite farther and snagged the hair clip.

"You heard right," he retorted even as he eyed the captivating rear view she'd presented him. As a rule, he preferred bodies by Venus. But that tight little tush and those American beauty legs more than compensated for what she lacked in voluptuous curves.

Suddenly seeing the wedding band on her finger, he set his still full beer bottle on the desk and spun away to retrieve the well log. He wasn't long on scruples, but he was loyal to one. Never with a married woman.

"Listen, lady," he needled her, dropping the drilling record on his desktop for emphasis, "I've got a lot of work to do and I'd really like to catch some Z's before I go back on tour..."

For just a fraction of a second Joni entertained the notion of telling him exactly where he could go. But she needed him. And though he didn't know it yet, he needed her.

She killed the notion and came to her feet, facing him squarely across the desk. "I've got a proposition for you."

He scanned her summarily, his eyes a wintry green. If she had the seven-year itch, she could damn well scratch it with someone else.

"A business proposition," she clarified, gleaning his thought.

He assumed an impatient stance. "Look—"

"No," she interrupted him, reaching into the pocket of the man's shirt she wore and pulling a rectangular card out for his inspection. "You look."

He gave her a lazy, amused smile. "A recipe card?"

She bridled at his mocking tone. "A map."

Intrigued in spite of himself, he looked a little closer at the fading pencil lines and saw that it was, indeed, a map.

"My grandmother drew it over fifty years ago," she explained, laying the card atop the open drilling log on the desk.

He cocked a cynical eyebrow. "Okay, lady, I give. What's this got to do with me?"

As briefly as possible then, Joni told him about that long-ago day when his grandfather had visited her grandfather's farm.

Chance McCoy stood perfectly motionless, but he felt a dizzying sense of deja vu. His grandfather, for whom he was named, had told him this very same story....

Like old soldiers and others who have walked the razor edge of danger, the oil witch had loved to reminisce. Many's the night he'd gotten into his cups and brought out choice fragments of memory, ornamenting them with imaginative details for his audience of one.

Black gold gushing a barrel a minute from the earth, boomtowns springing up overnight, oil rigs growing like sunflowers across the Oklahoma red beds—young

Chance had seen it all through his grand-father's eyes.

Just when it seemed that the sky was the limit, decreasing gas pressure and declining crude prices had brought on the bust. Debts piled up like dust, and the Great Depression that followed made panhandlers of million-aires and laughingstocks of oil spiritualists.

Those yarns—true in all the essentials but prettied up for the spinning—had fueled a burning ambition in the boy. Driven by the knowledge that the world is mainly depend-ent on exhaustible energy resources, and determined to redeem his grandfather's good name, he enrolled at Oklahoma University and earned a degree in geology.

Unfortunately, the oil witch died two weeks before commencement. Cirrhosis of the liver, his death certificate read. The night Chance graduated he got roaring drunk; the next morning he sobered up and signed on with an independent oil producer. If he wanted to be a wildcatter, he had to learn the business from the ground up.

He'd roughnecked for a while, working at every job from stabber to supervisor. Men who'd been riding the derricks down for more years than Chance was alive respected his degree but came to rely on his nose for oil. He could smell the stuff, they said, and that wasn't a skill that could be booklearned.

At the height of the oil and gas boom, he'd rounded up some investors and struck out on his own. He hit pay dirt his first time out, and there'd been few dry holes since.

Oil royalties rushed in like the tide, but the money was more the means to an end than an end in itself. Everywhere he drilled, from the Andarko basin to the Sandstone hills, he was following his elusive dream.

"How did you find me?" Chance demanded now.

"Believe me," Joni answered, "it wasn't easy."

As she explained how she'd tracked him down, driving from one drilling site to the next and pumping strangers for information, he shook his head in amazement.

"Remember," she said in summary, "all I had to work with was your grandfather's name and my grandfather's memories."

"That wasn't much to go on, considering the amount of time that's passed." He really had to admire her gumption. Given his erratic schedule the last few months, it was a wonder she hadn't thrown in the towel.

"I was ready to call it quits, when fate led me here."

"What do you mean?" His green eyes focused on her hands, and he wondered what kind of a sorry s.o.b. would let his wife work her fingers to the bone like that.

Not knowing what she'd done to earn his disdain, she looked down at her broken nails and skinned knuckles. All right, so she could use a manicure and a bottle of Jergens. But did he have to rub it in?

The silence lengthened, and Joni rushed to fill it. "After the banker rejected our application for a drilling loan, he said a man he didn't know from Adam had stopped by a couple of weeks before and told him our exact same story. Needless to say, you could've knocked me over with a toothpick when he showed us your business card. And when he told us you were drilling right here in Redemption County...as I said, fate led me here."

"Whatever's fair." Chance didn't believe in fate. Which was why he'd spent so much of his free time the last few years talking to small-town bankers and other old-timers who might have known his grandfather in his heyday. If he wanted to drill where the oil witch had dropped, he had to spread the word.

Clouds scudded through the blue skies of

her eyes as she glanced at the telephone on his desk. "I called the number on your business card nearly every day for two weeks, but I couldn't get past your answering machine."

"We've been working round the clock since we made hole." He recognized her husky twang from the tape, and he'd planned to call her back as soon as he got the time.

"This morning I climbed in my truck and told Grandpa I was going to find you or die trying." Her freckle-dusted nose wrinkled as she smiled triumphantly.

But he frowned, bothered by something she'd mentioned earlier. "Would you mind telling me why you were making application for a drilling loan?"

"To pay for casing and...such." She bit her lip, debating whether or not to elaborate, then left it at that.

"But the driller buys those things."

"That's what Jesse James said."

He stared at her with utter bemusement. "Jesse James?"

"One of Grandpa's nicer names for the banker." She felt ridiculously breathless when he returned her smile.

"What else did the robber baron tell you?" Chance's play on words reminded her of the problem at hand.

"That you'd pay us a landowner's royalty for drilling rights." Joni saw that she was going to break her barrette if she didn't quit playing with it, and stuck it into her jeans pocket.

"Three dollars an acre," he confirmed.

Her spirits dropped as she mentally multiplied their hundred and sixty acres by three. "But that's only four hundred and eighty dollars!"

"You also receive an overriding interest in the proceeds if the well is a producer," he pointed out.

She eyed him speculatively, thinking this was more like it. "What's an overriding interest worth?"

"One-eighth of the—"

"Moneywise, I mean."

"Mercenary one, aren't you?" His retort wounded her pride.

"I didn't drive all the way out here just to have you poke fun at me, Mr. McCoy." She reached for the recipe card. "If you won't take me seriously, I'll simply take my business elsewhere."

"Like hell you will." With the speed of summer lightning his hand lashed out and caught her wrist before she could grab the card. She had him over a barrel, and he knew she knew it. "What do you want from me, lady?"

"My name is Fletcher," she supplied with chilly dignity. "And I want a landowner's royalty of twenty thousand dollars."

"Twenty thousand dollars?!" His roar of disbelief thundered off the trailer walls.

She tried to pull her arm free; failing that, she went for broke. "I also want half the proceeds if our well is a producer."

His mouth tilted into another one of those sardonic smiles. "Our well, Mrs. Fletcher?"

She gave him tit for tat. "From where I'm standing, Mr. McCoy, my map and your money make it exactly that."

Furious to think she'd beaten him at his own game, he released her as suddenly as he'd grabbed her. "What do you think I am—a walking wallet?"

Fearing she'd pushed him too far, she decided to make a clean breast of it. "I know it's a lot to ask, but with our farm going under and Grandpa's medical bills piling up—"

His eyes sliced to her left hand, and her throat sealed over like a tomb. "What's the matter with your husband that he can't provide for his family?"

An anger that she hadn't even realized she

harbored suddenly raged inside her. But she shut the barn door on the forest fire of her emotions and dredged up her voice. "My husband is dead."

Chapter 2

Chance did a double-take that nearly tore his neck off. "What?"

"My husband is dead," Joni repeated, bracing herself for the obligatory "I'm sorry" that still, after all this time, left her lost for a reply.

"You led me to believe you were married," he said instead. "Widows wear their rings on their right hands, Mrs. Fletcher, not their left."

She knuckled away the tears that suddenly threatened and struck back venomously. "I don't need etiquette lessons, Mr. McCoy; I need twenty thousand dollars."

"Another farmer crying poormouth." he said snidely.

"Spoken like a true toolpusher," she said, exhausting her knowledge of driller's jargon with the vicious little jab.

"Come again?" he challenged her, smiling that killer smile.

"You can take the crude out of the ground," she returned sarcastically, "but you can't take the crude out of the—"

"I get the picture," he cut in roughly.

During the emotional meltdown across the desk, they'd begun to see each other in a new light. Now they took each other's measure.

If the truth be told, Chance liked everything he saw. The freckles gave her skin a velvety look that made his fingers tingle, while her generous mouth bespoke a woman of spirit.

His eyes dropped briefly to the chambray shirt that shrouded her slender frame, and he wondered if it might have belonged to her late husband. Whatever, she looked sexy as hell in the man-sized shirt.

It was her coloring that really intrigued him, though. With that bonfire of red hair and those sparkin' blue eyes, she reminded him of a wild well just begging to be tamed. And anyone with a lick of sense knew that was a challenge no "oilie" could resist.

Joni could feel the powerful drive of the drill bit shaking the trailer floor, touching off the craziest vibrations in the craziest places as she studied Chance with the same thoroughness he was using on her.

To her, he fit the mold of the independent oil man—a rough and ready gambler who played by his own rules. His form-fitting T-shirt displayed a sinuous body with long, fluid muscles that came from lifting pipe, not pumping iron. Years of working in the Oklahoma sun had tanned him to perfection.

Despite the rumpled black hair and the two-day growth of beard that shadowed his daredevil face, she couldn't help but notice the network of lines flanking his kinetic green eyes—lines that told her how often he laughed and how much he enjoyed the risky business of discovering oil.

Nor could she ignore the frankly sensual mouth that shocked her into realizing that her first impulse was to kiss him.

Guiltily she glanced down at her wedding band, remembering a June bride and her farm boy vowing to love, honor, and cherish "till death us do part." She strove to recall Larry's round, serious face, but her mind's eye refused to cooperate. All she could see was that dimly lit barn and a pair of scuffed work boots—

"How did he die?"

Joni raised her head in confusion, her three-year-old screams still echoing in her ears. "I beg your pardon?"

"Your husband." Chance had a gut feeling the guy had done a real number on her. "How did he die?"

"What difference does it make?" She

swallowed hard, drowning out those horrible screams. If only she could eliminate the nightmares that easily. "Larry's gone and you're my last hope."

He started to tell her not to go pinning her hopes or anything else on him—he had enough trouble without that. But before he could speak the door opened, admitting all the outside noise and an oil-smeared Tex.

"Good news, boss," the roughneck said to Chance. "We've found the pay in the Redfork formation."

Chance welcomed the interruption as much as he did the news. Maybe more. He picked up the drilling record and got down to business. "Let's get a sample and get it logged."

"Right," Tex replied.

Joni could feel the sudden charge in the air. It was as if a hot wire had just sent an electric spark through the trailer.

It seemed like eons since she'd been a part of something good, something exciting, and she would have given her eye teeth to stay and see what happened next. But fearing she would only be in the way, she reached for the recipe card that now lay on the desk.

"No."

The quiet command stopped her cold.

She drew her hand back quickly and looked curiously at Chance.

He gave the log to Alex. "Mrs. Fletcher and I have some unfinished business to take care of, so go ahead without me. You know what to do."

The roughneck's grin gleamed whitely in his blackened face as he reached to pull the door closed behind him. "Consider it done."

When he was gone, Chance picked up the card and carried it to the window, studying it intently in the lemony light that seeped through the blinds and trying to sort through feelings that had been a long time in coming.

It was a damned difficult thing to do, dividing past from present and separating emotion from experience. On the one hand, this could be the pot of gold at the end of that rainbow he'd been chasing; on the other hand, it could be the beginning of the end of his lifelong dream. Either way, he couldn't rush the process.

Until now, Joni had been too busy making her case to really size up the man she'd been searching high and low for. Given this breather, though, she realized she just might be getting in over her head.

He wore his hair a bit longer than was considered the fashion, as though he didn't give two hoots in hell what anybody else thought. But the black strands looked so springy and inviting, it took every ounce of willpower Joni possessed not to reach out and touch them.

She had a slim view of a profile that could have been carved by the restless wind, but mostly her view was restricted to his long, sinewy back. The heat had plastered his T-shirt to his muscled skin, making her conscious of the way his wall-to-wall shoulders tapered to a trim waist and taut buttocks.

He flipped the card over suddenly and read the other side, then turned to face her and asked, "Ever make it?"

"M—make what?"

"Buttermilk pie."

"Oh, no." Embarrassed by her momentary lapse, she hastened to clarify. "I got the card out of Grandma's apron pocket only a couple of months ago. See, she died giving birth to my daddy that day, and Grandpa had kept her things in the cedar chest in the attic. I didn't even know it existed until he sent me up there to dig it out."

A smile graced her lips as she studied the small card in his large hands. "I've been meaning to make one, but what with taking care of Grandpa, tending my tomatoes, and trying to find you, I haven't had time."

Chance took in her worn clothes and work-roughened hands, wondering when she found time for herself, and Joni realized she looked like something the cat dragged in.

Her blue chambray shirt had belonged to Larry. She'd stayed up late one night altering it down until it was only a couple of sizes too large for her. Her jeans were stiff with mud, and her waffle stompers...well, they'd seen better days.

As the silence thickened, she began twisting her wedding band in a nervous gesture that, for some reason, irritated the hell out of Chance.

"Tell me something," he demanded tersely. "How much life insurance did your husband have?"

She went pale as a ghost. "What's that got to do with our oil well?"

"You asked me for twenty thousand dollars, remember?" He felt like a real heel, putting her through this, but he had her dead to rights. "I'm just trying to make sure I won't be throwing good money after bad if I decide to drill on your land."

"If you doubt my integrity, Mr. McCoy—"

"You haven't answered my question, Mrs. Fletcher."

"Nor will I." She squared her narrow

shoulders determinedly and put her hand out, palm up. "Now, if you'll give me back my card, I'll get out of your hair."

Chance looked at her, all earth and fire and sky, and braved the elements with a smile. "You don't like me, do you?"

Joni had the grace to blush. "Let's just say that we don't have much in common and leave it at that."

"I think you're wrong," he challenged her laconically.

"I don't." She wiggled her fingers impatiently.

He kept the card firmly in hand. "You're aware, aren't you, that the oil industry is just now starting to come out of its worst price slump since the Depression?"

She kept a tight rein on her temper. "And you're aware that while the price of oil was going up to thirty dollars a barrel a few years back, the price of corn was going down to a dollar fifty a bushel?"

"You've had price supports."

"And you've had tax breaks."

He tried another tack. "The main reason I'm in business today is that I had enough revenue from my stripper wells to carry me over the hump."

She cut him off at the pass. "Well, the main

reason we quit growing corn last year is that we were losing fifty dollars an acre."

Their eyes met, and they engaged in a visual battle of wills that made their verbal skirmish seem tame by comparison.

Chance began to notice things about her that he hadn't noticed before. That her nose had an aristocratic bent, but her slightly squared jaw could have belonged to a pioneer. That her sadly neglected hands were as fragile and fine-boned as those of an ascetic. That for all her slight build, she had the heart of a fighter.

Little did he know that Joni was fighting her budding attraction to him as fiercely as she was fighting to save her farm.

He simply felt the determination radiating from her every pore and called a truce. "There's no use in our even discussing that twenty thousand dollars until I've run some tests on your land."

She dropped her hand but held her rising elation in check. "What kinds of tests?"

"Rock and soil samples, for starters."

"How long will that take?"

"A week." He shrugged those massive shoulders, causing his muscles to ripple beneath his T-shirt. "Two at the most."

"That's cutting it pretty close." She didn't

mean to sound pushy, but she was running out of time. "Our bank note comes due three weeks from today."

He looked down at the map, then up at her. "What are you doing tomorrow?"

She frowned. "Taking Grandpa to the doctor."

"What about Sunday?" Damn, but she had a sexy mouth—wide and curvy, with a lower lip that said she gave as good as she got.

Her frown segued into a smile. "Making a buttermilk pie."

"Sounds good to me." He flashed her a grin, revealing a set of strong white teeth, and they both laughed.

An ear-splitting hiss followed by a chorus of ribald curses told them he was needed on the rig floor.

He returned her card and reached for his hard hat. "No rest for the wicked."

She stuck out her hand. Catching sight of her chipped nails and chapped skin, she promptly withdrew it. "See you Sunday."

His beer bottle sat full and forgotten on the desk as he watched her walk to the door. It'd been a long time since a woman had captured his imagination and challenged his intellect. Longer still since a woman had commanded his respect.

"By the way, Mrs. Fletcher..."

Joni turned back reluctantly.

Chance surveyed the exquisitely feminine body beneath the man's shirt, rousing feelings between her blue eyes and jeans that she'd thought she'd buried forever.

"You were saying, Mr. McCoy?"

He cocked his hard hat at that rakish angle and gave her his rogue's gallery smile. "Remind me to show you just how much we have in common."

Chapter 3

"Hi."

"Hi."

Chance took off a pair of aviator sunglasses and stuck them into his jacket pocket as he crossed the porch. "It just occurred to me that I'm probably interrupting your dinner."

The clock in the entryway chimed the noon hour as Joni unhooked the screen door. "On the contrary, we decided to eat a little later today, thinking maybe you'd like to join us."

His swift stride slowed. "I hope you didn't go to any extra trouble on my account."

She made a tsking sound. "This from the man who tricked me into baking a buttermilk pie?"

His answering grin was totally unrepentant. "What do you say we skip dinner and go directly to dessert?"

Laughing now, she held the door open for him. "Come in and meet Grandpa."

He nodded. "Great."

Joni stood with her back against the doorjamb as he wedged himself past her. But still his body made brief contact with hers, and every cell went hot and cold with excitement.

At the same time, air raid sirens went off in her head. In a raw silk jacket, pale salmon polo shirt, and jeans, he looked no less dangerous than if he'd stormed her house wearing a curved scimitar in his belt and clutching a long-barreled rifle.

For his part, Chance was hard-pressed to reconcile this vision in soft blue jersey with the woman who'd visited him at the drilling site.

Her wild Irish hair had been tamed into a topknot, which made her freckles seem more pronounced and her eyes even larger than before. The open collar of her simple shirt-waist dress paid homage to that Botticelli neck, while its gently full skirt draped those fine filly legs.

And considering the state of her hands, it came as a real surprise to find toenails the color of pink tea roses playing hide-and-seek with the straps of her white sandals.

Which reminded him...

Joni saw that he'd zeroed in on her wedding band and she began fiddling with it, turning it round and round on her finger as she said, "Grandpa's waiting for us in the living room, Mr. McCoy."

Chance knew damned good and well she

was hiding behind that ring, but he let it ride for the moment. "After you, Mrs. Fletcher."

The peeling paint on the exterior of the farmhouse had spoken with sad eloquence about her struggle to make ends meet, but inside she had created an environment seemingly untouched by either tragedy or time.

Sunshine streamed in through two leaded glass windows that wore a vinegar-and-water sparkle. Between them, and behind a cherry settee that looked as if it dated from the Civil War era, a crazy quilt hung artfully on the wall. Pine plank flooring added its own glow. A ceiling fan provoked a cool breeze; come winter, the fieldstone fireplace would provide warmth.

A scarecrow of a man in Big Smith overalls and a faded plaid shirt pushed himself up by the armrests of an overstuffed club chair that had been the ultimate in comfort in the 1930s.

"Keep your seat, sir," Chance said as he crossed the room.

Bat Dillon's breath came hard and fast and difficult, but he didn't know the meaning of quit. "The day I can't stand to greet a guest is the day they can lay me in my grave."

Chance laughed and stuck out his hand, feeling an instant kinship with the feisty old codger. "You must be Grandpa."

"What's left of him," the old man confirmed, proffering his own knobby hand.

After making the introductions, Joni gave the recipe card to Chance and then went to the kitchen to fix them all some iced tea.

The pork steaks she planned to cook for dinner were thawing on the countertop, and the buttermilk pie she'd baked that morning was cooling on a wire rack. Much to her surprise, she caught herself humming a tune she'd heard on the radio as she arranged their glasses and spoons and the sugar bowl on a japanned tray.

She paused in the living room doorway, her heart as full as her hands when she saw how well the two men were getting along. Most of Grandpa's friends were either dead or dying, and except for his weekly appointment with Dr. Rayburn, he rarely left the house.

Even if Chance McCoy decided not to drill for oil, Joni thought as she rejoined them, the ear-to-ear grin on Grandpa's face right now more than rewarded her efforts to bring them together.

Chance looked up when she came in, then leapt up from the other club chair and reached for the tray. "Here, I'll take that."

Their eyes met during the exchange, and she stood there, flushing beneath his heavy-lidded regard, short of breath and totally flummoxed by her schoolgirl reaction.

He turned away and set the tray on the marble-topped table that separated the chairs, then turned back and gave her a glass.

This time they bumped hands, and she felt a growing warmth spreading up her arm, thawing nerves that had lain as dormant as seeds under the frozen earth.

"Chance was just saying that he likes to restore antique cars." Grandpa took a sip of his tea, seemingly oblivious to the high-octane tension building between the widow and the wildcatter. "I told him how I'd kept my tin lizzie, thinking Larry might want to tinker with it, but that he wasn't much of a car buff."

The use of her late husband's name knocked Joni for a loop. Knowing that if she didn't sit down she'd probably fall down, she perched on the edge of the settee and said the first thing that came to mind. "That's a fairly expensive hobby, isn't it?"

"Depends on how you define expensive." Chance reclaimed his chair and crossed an ankle over a knee, his polished Lucchese boots a galling reminder that not everybody in the room had a foreclosure notice hanging over their head.

"What do you think that old tin lizzie is worth today?" Grandpa asked.

"A damn sight more than you paid for it," Chance said, his smile on full beam now.

Joni looked at Grandpa, aghast. "Surely you're not considering selling such an important link with your past?"

He shrugged those coat-hanger shoulders. "What good's it doing me, sitting in the machine shed and going to rust?"

Chance let his head loll sideways. "I'd be glad to take a gander at it and give you an estimate."

"Is this how you acquire your antique cars, Mr. McCoy?" Joni glared accusingly at him.

His gaze skimmed over her in swift appraisal, making her feel defensive when she had absolutely nothing to feel defensive about. "When I see something I want, Mrs. Fletcher, I let my checkbook do the talking."

"Money doesn't always say the right thing," she replied with a touch of asperity.

"The only thing *my* money ever says is goodbye," Grandpa grumbled.

Chance's face was solemn, his eyes dancing as he raised his glass in a mock toast. "I'll drink to that."

Joni didn't even crack a smile. "Which brings us back to the original purpose of this meeting."

Chance explained the criteria he used for selecting a drilling site. He also discussed the rock and soil samples he planned to send to the state for analysis, but he made no mention of his long-held dream of redeeming his grandfather's name. That was nobody's business but his own.

"Any questions?" he asked a few minutes later.

Grandpa cleared his throat. "How about some more tea?"

"I'll second that," Chance agreed.

Joni left the living room with three empty glasses and a headful of fantasies about how she was going to spend all that money when her oil well came in. On returning, though, she realized one of her worst fears.

"What happened?" Her heart plunged sickeningly to her stomach when she found Chance standing solicitously over a wheezing Grandpa.

"Coughing spell."

"I'll get his medicine."

Guilt stalked her to the downstairs bathroom and back. "I should have known this would be too much excitement for him," she said to Chance after she made sure Grandpa swallowed his pills, and his breathing returned to normal.

But Chance was having none of that. "A little excitement never hurt anyone."

"This spell could have killed him."

"Then he would have died a happy man."

As much as Joni wanted to argue the point, she couldn't. The wildcatter's presence was the shot in the arm that Grandpa had needed for months. As for her own needs...

Elbowing the thought aside—a move she'd perfected during four years of marriage— she said, "Maybe he should rest a spell before dinner."

"All right." Chance didn't press his advantage. He just picked Grandpa up with the ease of a man used to physical labor and followed her into the dining room.

"I moved the sofa sleeper in here so he wouldn't have to climb the stairs," she explained as she closed the shutters at the windows and folded back a top sheet that smelled of fresh air and sunshine.

Chance laid Grandpa on the bed, his gentle hands belying his hard-bitten reputation, then took a good look around him. The huge mahogany table stood flush against the far wall to make room for the sofa, while the matching Windsor chairs stood stolidly in the four corners.

"Don't tell me you moved all this by yourself?" he asked incredulously.

"Don't tell me you still buy that old saw about women being the weaker sex?" she countered.

"Let me put it this way." he said, a slow smile kindling in his eyes when she leaned over to place a kiss on Grandpa's weathered cheek. "I've yet to meet a woman who didn't have it in her power to bring a man to his knees."

Joni could feel the heat of his gaze moving leisurely up the backs of her legs and over her jersey-clad derriere. She straightened, spun around, and caught him staring at her.

"Dinner will be ready in an hour, Mr. McCoy."

As she led him from the shuttered dining room into the sun-splashed living room, he noticed she wasn't wearing a slip. What she didn't realize, and what he was in no hurry to point out to her, was that when she passed in front of the window her skirt was entirely transparent.

"I want to talk to you, Mrs. Fletcher."

She checked to be sure Grandpa was resting comfortably before closing the doors between the two rooms. "What about?"

He hitched his chin toward the porch. "Let's go out there."

The instant they stepped outside, that devilish wind whipped Joni's jersey dress high above her knees. Chance drank in an eyeful of thigh as smooth as Tennessee whiskey. He'd known her legs were good... He just hadn't known how good.

"Don't you have anything better to do than to stand there gawking at me?" she fumed as she fought her whirling skirts.

He lazed back against the porch railing as if he had all the time in the world and crossed his arms over that acre of chest. "Nope."

"You said you wanted to talk to me," she reminded him starchily.

His eyes glided up her body, revealing none of his thoughts while seeming to take in everything about her. "How long has your grandfather had farmer's lung disease?"

Mercifully, the wind died down at that moment. Joni stopped battling her skirt and sought refuge in the old oak porch swing that Grandpa had built with younger, stronger hands. "How did you know?"

Chance shrugged, those strapping shoulders straining the seams of his silk jacket.

"I've drilled some water wells for farmers, and about half of them have his same symptoms."

She stared off into the distance. But she was looking backward now, not forward. "I remember his spells starting the year that black dust covered our wheat. We had a really good stand that year, but the dust ruined..."

Her voice snagged on the memory, and she coughed to clear it. "I took care of all the chores around here while Grandpa and Larry worked day and night, trying to save what they could. But with no cab on the combine, they'd come in from the fields just coated with the stuff."

"Did Larry die of farmer's lung disease?"

"No," she answered shortly, and that was all she intended to say.

Chance hesitated, knowing his next question could open a real can of worms. But he needed the information for the purpose of drawing a contract if he decided to drill. "Whose name is on the deed to this farm?"

"Grandpa's and mine, as joint tenants." Joni gave the porch floor a nudge with her heel, setting the swing in motion, then folded her hands in her lap. "You look surprised."

"Curious is more like it."

She saw a small patch of beard near his

right sideburn that had escaped the morning razor, and it provoked an unsettling feeling of intimacy. "How so?"

His brows were pulled down into a low V over his eyes. "I'm just wondering why you haven't put the farm in your name and put your grandfather on Medicaid."

"Farmers want parity, Mr. McCoy, not charity."

"That's all well and good, Mrs. Fletcher, but it sounds like you're letting pride get in the way of practicality."

She lifted her chin a notch. "Meaning..."

Looking down at her freckled face, seeing the soft violet shadows of fatigue that lay under her beautiful blue eyes, Chance felt something stir deep inside him. Something he chose to ignore in light of what had to be said.

"Meaning you could put your grandfather in a nursing home and get on with the business of making this place pay."

Joni's lips parted as if he'd just plunged a knife between her ribs. For a moment she didn't speak, but only stared at him. When she did find words, her voice underscored her contempt for the root of her problems.

"And you called me a mercenary!" She stopped the swing and surged to her feet, advancing on him with the ferocity of a spring cyclone. "Well, let me tell you something, you—you money-grubbing bastard! Grandpa was born here and he's going to die here."

Standing toe to toe with the wildcatter now, she jabbed that Rock of Gibraltar chest with an emphatic finger. "This is the only home he's ever known, and as long as I've got breath in my body, no one is going to take it from him. Or him from it!"

Chance took a real pounding as she blew her course. And when she'd spent her fury, he took her in his arms.

Joni tried to resist. She raised her hands to his shoulders, thinking to push him away, reminding herself that he was a rolling stone...here today, gone tomorrow.

But her need to be held overrode the restraints of her mind, and she latched onto him as if there were no tomorrow. He was here. And for now that was all that mattered.

Chance gathered her close, expecting a deluge, but Joni came up dry-eyed and horribly embarrassed at having been caught with her defenses down.

"I'm sorry." With a quick twist she slipped free of his hold and turned to look over the

51

fields that should have begun greening with wheat and corn and milo by now. "I don't know what got into me, lighting into you one minute and then throwing myself at you the next."

"No harm done." If she could shrug it off, so could he. But there was no denying that she'd felt more womanly than any other woman he'd ever held in his arms.

Oddly deflated by his indifferent tone, she took a deep, restorative breath. "Was there anything else you wanted to discuss with me, Mr. McCoy?"

"Chance."

"I beg your pardon?"

He saw her shoulder blades draw pointedly erect under that clingy material. "My name is Chance."

The wind picked up again, and she clamped her skirt down with palms suddenly gone clammy. "So?"

"So I want to hear you say it."

"Why?"

"Come on, Joni." His use of her name made her blood sing. As did his touch when he took her by the arm and turned her so that her back was to the wind, his face into it. "Just say Chance."

She sensed that to give an inch with this

man was to give a mile, but she relented anyway. "Chance."

"Very good." A smile tinged his tempting lips as he released her and reached into his jacket pocket for the recipe card that mapped their mutual dreams. "Now that we're on a first-name basis, you can say 'Good luck, Chance,' and I can say 'Thank you, Joni,' and—"

"Mr. McCoy—"

"Chance."

"Chance," she repeated softly.

"Again," he demanded.

She bowed her head as chills having nothing to do with the brisk spring breeze chased along her spine.

He slid a callused finger under her chin and brought her head up, forcing her to look at him.

Like magnets of opposite charge, their eyes met. "Good luck, Chance."

"Thank you, Joni."

An emotion that neither dared name crackled between them.

Chance dropped his hand, satisfied for now. "I'll be back in an hour, maybe less."

Joni nodded her head, but she couldn't shake the memory of his touch. "I'll have dinner waiting."

~ ~ ~

Dammit all to hell, he couldn't concentrate!

Chance stood motionless in the cornfield, his nose to the wind but his mind on a woman with legs that wouldn't quit and a wedding band that stopped him cold.

Normally, this was the easy part of his job. There was no explaining it, really, except to say that sometimes the sulfuric odor filled his nostrils and sometimes it didn't. But how in the Holy B. Hell was he supposed to smell oil when he still had a headful of *her* ninety-nine-and-forty-four-one-hundredths-percent-pure soap?

Joni. She'd lost her husband, her farm was going the way of the wind, and her grandfather didn't look or sound like he was long for this world. Yet she refused to cry. Refused to give up. Sadder still, she refused to let go.

He thought he caught a trace of sulfur in the air, but he couldn't be sure. Changing positions, he shoved back both front panels of his silk jacket and stood with hands on hips and feet braced apart, his face to the limitless sky.

What a joke...Here he'd spent fifteen of his thirty-five years trying to salvage his grandfather's name. And now that he was only a whiff away from making the old man look good, what did he do? He just stood there like some horny teenager, thinking with his glands instead of his brains.

Joni, Joni. She had a beautiful mass of hair, too many freckles to count, plus the gorgeous legs. A pretty enticing package. But what man in his right mind wanted to compete with a memory?

He could have sworn he smelled it now, the acrid sting of sulfur. He closed his eyes and inhaled deeply, waiting for the noxious fumes to set his nostrils and lungs afire.

The red wind blew, dusting his hair and clothes and dulling the shine on his boots. A giant tumbleweed, dry and gnarled, rolled ahead of it. For all he noticed, it could have been the calmest day since Creation.

He opened his eyes and exhaled on a savage curse, still not certain. This had never happened to him before. But then, he'd never been this close to grabbing the brass ring before either.

Maybe he was too uptight. Too eager to prove his grandfather right. Maybe the map was wrong. That was a real possibility. Maybe he should cut his losses and hit the road before he made a costly mistake.

A red-tailed hawk drifted through the sky in ever-widening circles. He watched it for a moment and then he made his decision. Screw the money, he was going for it. For himself, for two old men who'd dared to dream, and for...

Joni. He turned on his heel and headed back to the house. She wasn't his type, so just why the hell did he want her?

~ ~ ~

Lord love a duck, she'd forgotten her slip!

Joni's face turned as red as her hair when she found her half slip lying on her bed. She'd run upstairs to close the windows, wanting to keep the dust from blowing in, and...

Looking down, she realized she could see right through her skirt. No wonder Chance had smiled at her like that.

She snatched up her slip and stepped into it, remembering now how she'd happened to forget it.

Just after daybreak she'd gone out to weed and water her tomatoes. Then she'd hosed off and come in to cook breakfast and make her buttermilk pie. Grandpa had been talky as a jaybird, partly due to the prednisone he was taking and partly due to the excitement of having company. So she'd lingered with him over a second cup of coffee.

When all was said and done, she'd barely had enough time for a shower and shampoo. In fact, she'd been standing in the upstairs bathroom in her underwear and sandals, putting the finishing touches on her hair, when she'd heard Chance pull into their gravel driveway. Rather than make Grandpa get up and go to the door, she'd grabbed her dress on the run, buttoning it up as she dashed downstairs to greet him.

Now, drawn by something beyond her ken, she went back to the window and saw Chance coming toward the house. She started to turn away, then changed her mind and stood there for a moment.

Lean and light on his feet, he moved with the quick confidence of a man who was used to taking charge. Watching from above, she couldn't help but remember how Larry had always plodded in from the fields as though he were carrying the weight of the world on his back.

Another difference loomed large in her mind. The thought brought an immediate backlash of guilt, but there was no ignoring it. Chance's arms had made her feel secure in a way that Larry's never had. Maybe it was because Larry had always been a little awkward about showing physical affection. More likely yet, it was all those years of frustration and fear catching up with her.

Confusing feelings welled up inside her as she turned away from the window. She didn't need to see the two men side by side to realize they were exact opposites in every respect but one. Larry had built up her hopes, then broken her heart. If she let him, Chance would too.

"Now, this is what I call larrupin' good," Grandpa declared later as he reached for another biscuit.

That he'd managed to make it to the kitchen table on his own had been miracle enough for Joni. But to see him take a second helping when he normally only picked at the first one brought a new and happy stinging to her eyes.

She blinked to keep the tears at bay and looked at Chance, who sat across the table from her. "You don't like okra?"

Truth was, he wasn't overly fond of fuzzy food. He didn't want to seem impolite, though, so he forked up one of the lightly seasoned, dark green pods and put it in his mouth. Amazingly, he found it both tender and tasty.

He swallowed and shot her a surprised grin. "I guess I do."

"Pass the gravy, please." Grandpa grabbed the top and bottom of his biscuit with gnarled hands, gave it a gentle tug, and pulled it apart. A haze of buttermilk-scented steam rose from each ragged half as he placed them on his plate.

Joni and Chance reached for the gravy boat at the same time. Their fingers coupled in the china crook, their gazes connected, and she felt as if she'd just received a billion-volt shock. Yanking her hand away, she let him have the gravy boat and picked up the empty meat platter instead.

"I'll get some more pork steaks." It was a perfectly ordinary statement, yet her voice sounded strange—as if her vocal cords had begun fraying. Scraping her chair back, she stood and crossed to the stove, acutely aware of those magnetic green eyes following her every move.

At least he couldn't see through her skirt, she told herself smugly as she opened the oven and dished up the rest of the meat. But she couldn't help wondering what he'd thought of her legs.

Her red hair and long legs were her best features, and while she appreciated them now, she'd hated them with a passion when she was growing up. Like most children, she'd placed a high premium on conformity. She'd been different enough, having lost her parents in that car wreck with a drunken driver. Being an orphan with carroty hair and matchstick legs had seemed triply unfair. And her freckles...lordy, as a teenager she'd tried everything from bleaching agents to lemon wedges to teas applied with a cotton pad to get rid of them. Nothing had worked, of course. And now, at twenty-nine and holding, she simply considered them good camouflage for any fine lines she'd begun collecting.

Closing the oven door, Joni turned back to the table feeling uncomfortable under the impact of Chance's stare. He'd been studying her from behind, his green eyes as unblinking as a great cat's, and she knew that he knew she was wearing her slip.

"Here you go." She handed the meat platter to Grandpa in order to avoid a repeat performance with Chance and resumed her chair.

"I think I'll pass." Grandpa gave the platter to Chance. "After that last biscuit, I'll be lucky if I can do justice to a piece of that buttermilk pie."

She laughed and placed an affectionate palm against his leathery cheek. "You have eaten better than usual today."

Chance speared his second crispy-tender pork steak, then offered the platter to Joni. When she shook her head no, he set it in the middle of the table and took another biscuit.

"More okra?" she asked teasingly.

It was hard to say whom he surprised the most, himself or her, when he answered, "Don't mind if I do."

She passed him the vegetable bowl and they smiled at each other as if they'd just shared some silly private joke.

"This is the best meal I've had in a month of Sundays," he proclaimed as he ladled thick creamy gravy over the cleaved biscuit.

"Joni won three blue ribbons at the county fair for her cooking," Grandpa remembered proudly.

She squirmed uncomfortably in her chair. "That was a long time ago."

"The summer you and Larry got married, as I recall," he went on musingly.

A lifetime ago. She stood, spurred to action by a sudden burst of anger, and began clearing the table. Before she realized what she was doing, she'd even snatched Chance's plate right out from under his nose.

"Joni!" Grandpa's jarring reprimand served to clear the fog of fury and confusion that had enveloped her.

She stopped just short of scraping everything into the dog's dish, whirled away from the sink, and met Chance's somber expression. He'd taken off his jacket before joining them at the table, and his pale shirt played up his perfectly bronzed skin and powerful build.

"I'm sorry," she said as her rage ebbed away and embarrassment flooded in to fill the void. It certainly wasn't his fault that she'd only just begun to deal with her feelings of having been betrayed. "Would you like your plate back?"

He eyed the lopsided mess she'd made of his dinner and shook his head. "Go ahead and give it to the dog."

"Tell you what," she said, setting his ruined plate aside and reaching for a paper sack to fill with the untouched leftovers, "I'll fix you a people bag."

He smiled, pleased. "Now that's one offer I won't refuse. I eat out most of the time, so it's liable to be a cold day in July before I get biscuits like that again."

"Not necessarily," Grandpa refuted.

Two pairs of puzzled eyes veered in the old man's direction.

A grin plied the gullies at the corners of his mouth. "I was just thinking, now that Chance has decided to drill, we can put him up."

"What are you—a mind reader?" Chance hadn't said word one about his plans and was surprised by the old codger's perception.

By tacit agreement they'd deferred their business discussion until dinner was over and done with, but Joni could see that dessert would have to wait.

"Put him up?" she repeated, staring at Grandpa as though he were crazy. "You mean have him move in here?"

"It's the least we can do, considering what he's going to do for us." His grin widened and the gullies changed courses. "And now that I'm sleeping downstairs, he can have my room."

Which was directly across the hall from *her* room.

Grandpa eyed her expectantly, his skeletal face more animated than she'd seen it in months. "So what do you say?"

"I..." Joni realized the bind she was in. Grandpa was starved for companionship, and the groundwork for a lasting friendship between the two men had already been laid. But she didn't want to spend every night just a hop, skip, and a jump away from

Chance McCoy. He was much too virile, and she was much too vulnerable.

She couldn't say that, of course, so she passed the buck to Chance, hoping against hope it would stop right there. "I thought you lived in your trailer."

Grandpa snorted in disgust. "That boar's nest?"

"Boar's nest!" Chance looked at her, affronted. "Is that how you described my trailer—a boar's nest?"

Her face turned bright red, but she refused to back down. "Would you rather I'd have said pigsty?"

"Six of one, half dozen of the other," Grandpa noted.

"That bad, huh?" Chance asked her abashedly.

Joni nodded solemnly. "That bad."

"Well, now that that's settled," Grandpa said, "I'd like a piece of pie and a cup of coffee."

But it wasn't settled. Not by a long shot. And as Joni cut the pie and poured the coffee, she wondered if it was too late to call a locksmith.

~ ~ ~

Chance glanced at the sky, surprised to see how dark it had gotten, then stuck his sunglasses into his jacket pocket. "Guess I won't be needing them after all."

Joni wrapped her arms around the wooden porch support that ran from railing to roof and laid her cheek against its cool surface. "Thanks for helping me get Grandpa into bed. He likes you a lot."

"Listen—" He stopped on the second step down and turned back, at eye level with her now. "I'm sorry for what I said this afternoon about putting him in a nursing home. He's lucky to have you."

"Kin-keeping is sort of a family tradition." She smiled to see how his hair blended with the backdrop of sky. "He raised me after my folks died, so I'm just returning the favor."

It was a windless night—a rare blessing in Redemption—and the land was so full of silence that there was no room for sound. The moon, aided by a million stars, spilled silvery light over the barren fields that stretched to the horizon.

But were they really barren, Joni wondered now, or did they hold a bellyful of crude? She wouldn't know the answer to that until Chance drilled a test well, something he planned to do as soon as he put the well he'd brought in the other day on pump.

She almost laughed out loud, remembering how Grandpa's jaw had dropped open when Chance said he was going to send them a check for twenty thousand dollars along with a lease agreement requiring their notarized signatures.

They'd been sitting out here. Grandpa and she in the swing and Chance in the wicker rocker, talking about the oil witch and discussing the various aspects of the drilling schedule. On hearing about the money, Grandpa had gotten so excited that she'd thought sure he was going to fall out of the swing and onto the floor.

Unfortunately, he'd gotten too excited for his own good. And the memory of him bowing forward suddenly and hammering at the early evening air with a cough reminiscent of machine-gun fire turned her smile upside down.

"He'll be fine by morning," Chance said in the moonlit silence, thinking her face was so lovely and so expressive. He hated seeing her frown.

"I hope so." Joni cleared her throat and broached the subject that had been bothering her since dinner. "He's bound and determined that you're going to move in here, you know."

That cynical eyebrow shot up like an inky caret mark. "And you're bound and determined to keep me out."

"Yes," she answered truthfully, "I am."

"Why?" He planted a booted foot on the porch floor and crossed his forearm over his thigh, leaning toward her.

"I'm afraid you'll hurt him." She let go of the wooden post and took a step backward, feeling a need to put some distance between them. "I'm afraid he'll come to depend on you, maybe even to love you. And when you leave—"

"You can go to hell for lying same as you can for stealing, Joni."

"I don't know what you're talking about."

"You're not afraid I'll hurt your grandfather." Chance stepped all the way up onto the porch now, enveloping her in his moonshadow. "You're afraid I'll hurt you."

"That's ridiculous!" She put up a brave front, but she was a regular bundle of nerves.

"Is it?" He moved forward slowly, like an animal sensing the presence of his quarry.

Her back was to the screen door now, and the light shining out from the ceiling fixture in the hallway burnished his copper skin with gold. "Wh-what are you going to do?"

"What do you think I'm going to do?" He

stopped and braced his hands on the wooden doorframe, leaving her no avenue of escape.

She folded her elbows tightly between them and tucked her fists partway under her chin. "I...I think you're going to kiss me."

Chance lowered his head so that his mouth was just a breath away from hers. Leaned inward so that Joni could feel his heat and his hardness through her thin jersey dress. Dropped his slumberous eyelids to half mast so that he could see—.

Her wedding ring.

"Not now," he whispered against her trembling lips. "But soon."

The night breathed the rich musk of all its gathered springs, all its beginnings and endings, as he eased away from her. In the distance a mockingbird trilled its regrets. Even the wind sputtered a mild protest.

Joni looked down at that cold band of gold encircling her finger, then up at the bold lines of Chance's face.

"I'll let you know when I'm moving in," he said before turning on his heel and bounding down the porch steps.

She mashed her fingers against her hungry lips, realizing suddenly that the card he carried with him was a recipe for trouble.

Chapter 4

Chance moved in on the following Sunday, and by the next Saturday, Joni was ready to move out.

For one thing, he took up too much space.

It wasn't that he was inordinately proportioned, though he certainly had an imposing presence. He stood six feet tall in his socks and weighed one hundred eighty pounds in his skivvies. And she knew for a fact that there wasn't an ounce of flab on his flatly muscled frame.

But when he came indoors, he brought the outdoors with him. The wind clung to his hair like a lover. His skin smelled of sunshine—salty and stimulating. Those expansive shoulders shrank doorways, and that earthy laughter shook rafters. Sometimes she had to leave a room when he entered it because there didn't seem to be enough oxygen for the two of them.

And for another, he upset her usual routine.

Monday, she'd gotten up at just after daybreak, as she always did, and accidentally walked in on him in the upstairs bathroom.

There he'd stood, all sunburned brawn, his shirt off and his jeans only partially zipped. And there she'd stood, wearing nothing but her nightgown and a rosy blush, involuntarily intrigued by that inverted triangle of hair that worked its way downward.

Wednesday he'd spent the whole afternoon tinkering with the old tin lizzie. She'd been doing both her bookwork and her darnedest to ignore him. Try as she might, though, she couldn't ignore the constant clanging in the machine shed. And when she found herself adding the same column of figures three times and coming up with three different answers, she'd put her ledgers away.

Last night Chance and Grandpa had stayed up until all hours, laughing and talking and playing pitch. Joni had excused herself and gone to bed with a farm journal. But instead of reading for a while and then turning off the light as she normally did, she'd lain alone in her double bed wishing she'd joined in on the fun.

Fun. She couldn't really remember the last time she'd had any. Not that she was feeling sorry for herself, for heaven's sake. She'd chosen to continue the fight after Larry died, and hard times or no, she didn't regret her decision.

She loved this land, and she lived for the challenge of planting a seed and watching it grow, nurturing it through inclement weather and ruinous clouds of insects as she might have nursed a child through minor colds and the painful throes of adolescence.

Even if the corn no longer marched as straight and tall as a row of soldiers toward the horizon, she still had her tomato beds and a contract with that food broker in Oklahoma City who shipped fresh vegetables nationwide. Next year maybe she'd even have enough revenue from her oil wells to experiment with that new variety of seed she'd seen advertised.

But now, with a week of hard work behind her and Saturday night looming up like—

"Joni?"

"Chance!" Her heart slammed against her rib cage as she spun away from the porch railing, and she didn't know whether it was because he'd startled her or because he looked good enough to eat in his clean white shirt and neatly pressed jeans. "I thought you were going to town with the guys tonight."

He eased the screen door shut behind him so as not to wake Grandpa and closed the gap between them in two long strides. "I was planning to until Tex mentioned something about a dance out at the cross-roads—whatever the hell that is."

Remembering what had happened the last time they were alone out there, Joni edged toward the safety of the swing. "It means just what it says."

Picking up on her discomfiture, Chance leaned a shoulder indolently against the porch support. "You mean it's an intersection? A real live crossroads?"

"About two miles west of here," she said, and sat. He looked in that direction, and twilight limned the rugged lines of his forehead, nose, and lips. "Have you ever been there before?"

"My girlfriend, Loretta West, and I used to go every Saturday night." She folded her hands in her lap and laced her fingers tightly together. For reasons she couldn't define, she felt terribly restless tonight.

"What about you and Larry?"

"He didn't like to dance."

His eyes found hers in the dusk. "Wanna go again?"

"What?" Joni couldn't have been more surprised if he'd asked her to sprout wings and fly.

"You heard me." Chance took a cigarette and a silver lighter inlaid with turquoise out of his shirt pocket. He never smoked in the house, in deference to Grandpa's condition. But if he didn't keep his hands busy right now, he wasn't sure he could keep them off of her.

She studied his unsmiling face in the red-gold flame from his lighter, unaware that he harbored some serious doubts about their living arrangement himself.

He was too old to be spinning his wheels like this. That first morning, when she'd barged in on him in the bathroom, auburn hair a-tangle and blue eyes still dewy from sleep, it'd been all he could do not to lay her down right then and there.

They had agreed to take turns in the bathroom after that. He used it first in the morning since he had to leave, and she used it first at night since she liked to go to bed with the chickens. Yet every time he remembered how she'd looked in her short pink nightgown with its pretty lace trim, he went as hard as his hat.

And then there was that business of her leaving a room whenever he entered it. She was always casual about it, and she always had an excuse. But it was obvious to him, if not to Grandpa, that she was going out of her way to avoid him.

Grandpa. Now, there was a survivor if he'd ever met one. The poor old guy had lost his wife in childbirth, his son and daughter-in-law in a tragic accident, and over half his breathing capacity to a freak of nature. One thing he hadn't lost was his fighting spirit, and he'd passed that along to his granddaughter.

Chance inhaled a goodly portion of smoke, wondering how in the hell he'd gotten himself into such a stupid predicament. Then he exhaled, thinking he'd just cancel the invitation and tell Joni that he was moving back to the trailer tomorrow morning.

She beat him to the punch. "Thanks for asking me, but I haven't been dancing in so long, I'm afraid I've forgotten how."

Why he didn't grab the out she'd offered him and run with it, he couldn't say. But he found himself trying to persuade her to go with him. "Dancing is a lot like riding a bicycle. Once you learn, you never really forget how."

"I don't know." Part of her wanted to jump at the opportunity to get out of the house for a while, but the other part of her was afraid that accepting was the same as waving a red flag in front of a bull.

"C'mon," he cajoled her, his eyes gleaming

their lazy way down her gingham blouse and blue jeans. "Get your glad rags on and go with me."

The cicadas chirped anxiously, echoing her heartbeat. But still, she hesitated. "What if Grandpa wakes up and needs something?"

"While you're getting dressed," he said, "I'll call and ask Skinny to come over and stay with him."

Joni glanced toward the cornfield. Flood-lights illuminated the newly raised drilling rig and the trailer where the roughnecks were bunking. "He's not going to the cross-roads?"

"No."

"Why not?"

Chance chuckled. "Because the last woman he danced with charged him with assault and battery."

"What happened?" she asked, shocked.

"He attacked her with his two left feet."

She groaned and rolled her eyes in mock hopelessness. "What can I say?"

He took a last drag on his cigarette, then stubbed it out. "Try yes."

The shimmering silver of her laughter lit up the darkening sky. "All right already, yes."

He held the screen door open for her. "I'll check on Grandpa, and then I'll call Skinny."

She caught a drift of his pine soap as she slipped past him. "Meet you on the porch in twenty minutes?"

"I'll be there with bells on," he assured her.

Joni started up the staircase, then stopped and turned back to him. "By the way, did I tell you that Dr. Rayburn paid you quite a compliment yesterday?"

"Really?" Chance paused in the living room doorway. "What'd he say?"

She smiled. "That you're the best dose of medicine Grandpa's had in a long time."

"Hey, that's great," he said, flexing his shoulders and his dimples in heart-melting harmony.

Those dimples made her panic, and she wondered if it was too late to break their— She shied away from the word *date,* but she couldn't think of another to substitute.

He saw the shadow of doubt dimming her eyes and knew he'd better distract her before she tried to back out on him. "You never did tell me what happened at the bank."

"The bank?" Her tone implied it was the furthest thing from her mind. "What about the bank?"

He shrugged, sending all sorts of muscles into play. "I was just wondering how Jesse

James reacted when you made your mortgage payment almost two weeks early."

"Oh." She couldn't suppress a small smile at the memory. "Well, when he finished picking himself up off the floor, he agreed to extend our other notes until our oil well comes in."

This talk about the loan started Joni thinking again about the farm.

Like most farmers, they were in debt up to their ears. During the boom years, inflation at home and a weak dollar abroad had sent crop prices and land values skyrocketing. At the urging of economists and government officials alike, they'd planted fencerow to fencerow, borrowing money to buy seeds and fertilizer and diesel fuel on land that had been in the family since the opening of the Cherokee Strip.

She remembered how the bust had caught them completely off guard. One day the banker was telling them the sky was the limit, and the next, he was calling in their loans. She'd never forget that day.

Grandpa, while shaken, had taken it pretty much in stride. Joni had taken it better than she'd thought possible. But Larry...Larry had taken it hard.

To keep the bank from foreclosing, they'd

sold off two hundred acres and all their live-stock. Each sale was like an amputation. But the money helped reduce their debt, which in turn made them eligible for an emergency loan that allowed them to start planting.

With their hearts in their throats, they'd prayed the worst was behind them. It wasn't. The dollar was growing stronger, drying up the foreign markets. When food originally meant to be shipped overseas began to flood American stores, crop prices dropped through the floor. At the same time, the interest rate on their remaining loans climbed to twenty-two percent.

Although she couldn't discuss this with Chance, Joni couldn't keep the thoughts at bay. There was the day Grandpa had gone on the warpath, writing blistering letters to everyone from the president of the bank to the President of the United States. Then she had gone to work as a waitress at the local truck stop, making minimum wage plus tips. But Larry...Larry had gone off the deep end.

Now, three years after her husband had let her have it with both barrels, Joni had Chance to thank for renewing her faith in the future. And it was for that reason—and that reason alone, she told herself sternly—that she owed him her company tonight.

"Well," she said, breaking this stream of consciousness that had transported her back to unhappy times, "I guess I'd better get moving." And leave the past behind, she silently added.

"Guess so," he agreed, relieved to see the shadows leave her eyes and the light return. He hated it when she retreated into herself like that. Not only did it make him feel helpless as hell, but it twisted something deep inside his gut. And no woman had ever done that to him before.

Chance crossed to the bottom of the stairs and called up after her. "Joni?"

She pivoted, her youthful ponytail coming to rest over her left shoulder. "Yes?"

He tossed her a summer-wine smile that made her thirsty for more. "Leave your hair down tonight."

Chapter 5

Five minutes to shower, ten minutes to dry her hair and put on her makeup, and five minutes to get dressed. That left her no time to think about what she was doing, which was all for the better. Because if she'd stopped to think about it, she couldn't have gone through with it.

But as she descended the stairs exactly twenty minutes later, Joni got a full-blown case of the jitters. What if Chance didn't like her dress? Maybe applying makeup had been going too far. And an emery board and hand lotion. Why had she used them tonight when she hadn't used them in months? Months? Years!

She paused on the bottom step and wet her lips with the tip of her tongue, whether from dread or anticipation she couldn't honestly say. Then, drawing a deep breath in the hope of stilling her butterflies, she went to the screen door and peered out, looking for Chance.

He wasn't there.

She knew it. He'd changed his mind and

gone to the crossroads without her. Blinking dangerously fast now, she turned away from the door.

And saw the light in the kitchen.

The sound of laughter, Chance's as smooth as hot syrup and Grandpa's as gravelly as the driveway, lured her into that warm, inviting room. As she should have guessed, they were sitting at the table, finishing a game of pitch.

Joni hovered in the doorway as nervous as a squirrel's tail, while they gave her the once-over.

Her dress, a voile bouquet of lavender and blue, recaptured the romantic spirit of a bygone era. A lacy collar adorned the jewel neckline in front, then followed it on around to a plunging V-back. The slim self belt cinched her wisp of a waist, while the circle skirt swirled graciously to her shapely calves.

In keeping with Chance's request, she'd left her hair swinging free in a fiery cascade. And on her feet were the strappy white sandals he'd seen before.

"Whistle me 'Dixie'!" Grandpa exclaimed, laying his winning hand of cards aside. "Don't you look like summer's just around the corner."

Chance slapped his loser's quarter on the

table and smiled. "I couldn't have said it better myself."

Not until her lungs began to hurt did Joni realize she'd forgotten to breathe. Drawing in a deep gulp of air, she looked at Chance. "I'm ready whenever you are."

Grandpa scratched his sagging jaw. "Haven't I seen that dress somewhere before?"

"It belonged to Grandma." Joni had found it in the cedar chest in the attic when she'd gone up there to get the recipe card. She'd fallen in love with it on the spot. Perfectly preserved in blue tissue paper, it had needed only a few tucks in the bodice to make it fit her to a T.

Sadness tugged his face into strange folds. "Now I remember...Ruthann was wearing it the night that I proposed to her."

A prickle of guilt traced through Joni's veins. "If you'd rather I not wear it, just say so."

"Wear it, and anything else of hers you want, in good health, darlin'." His voice crackled like a dry leaf. "I think she'd be pleased as punch to know you're enjoying it."

"Thank you, Grandpa." Joni crossed to the kitchen table and kissed his wrinkled cheek.

He cleared his throat and picked up the playing cards. "Go on now, the both of you, and have fun."

"Sorry I woke you earlier," Chance said as he stood.

The old man shrugged. "I've got an eternity to sleep."

Chance gripped his shoulder with a gentle hand. "Skinny should be here in a few minutes."

Grandpa began stacking the deck, his milky blue eyes gleaming expectantly. "I'll be watching for him."

After extracting the old cardsharp's promise that he wouldn't take the young roughneck for too many quarters, Chance led Joni out to his car, a '56 Thunderbird convertible he'd restored to mint condition. Its hand-rubbed chrome stood out in shiny relief against its Fiesta Red body.

"Do you want me to put the top up?" he asked as he held the passenger door open for her.

"Not really." She tipped her head back and shook it. "I've never ridden in a convertible before."

Chance got in on the driver's side, his eyes crinkling in appreciation of the entrancing portrait she made in the brief flare of the floor light. "There's a scarf in the glove compartment if it gets too windy for you."

Joni kept her face to the night sky, telling herself it was ridiculous to feel jealous of all those other women who might have taken him up on the offer. One date, and she was ready to hogtie the guy! "I love the wind."

He inserted the key in the ignition. But instead of turning the engine on, he turned to her. "C'mere."

She rolled her head sideways in surprise. "What?"

He slid his right arm along the back of the seat and wrapped a wayward strand of her silky hair around his finger, pulling on it playfully. "No damn doorhuggers allowed in my car."

"You mean you want me to—"

"Haul your buns over here."

"But—"

"No buts, just buns."

"That's bad," she groaned, scooching over to sit hip to hip beside him.

"That's better," he declared, releasing her only long enough to start the engine and shift gears before draping his arm around her shoulders again.

Joni gave directions to the crossroads and Chance steered the convertible onto the highway, controlling it with one hand as well as most drivers control their cars with two.

The wind wreaked havoc with their hair and made conversation impossible. But each was so mindful of the other's presence, words would have been difficult to come by.

Chance kept his eyes on the road, but it was all he could do to keep his free hand from straying to her small breast, his fingers from strumming her slender neck. He wanted to find out for himself if that sweet mound of flesh felt as firm as it looked, if her skin was as soft and satiny as he imagined it...all over.

Joni sat primly, hands folded in her lap and knees together, but her thoughts ran wild and free. Every time he took a curve, causing her to lean closer to him, she wondered what it would be like to have that muscular torso crushing her into the mattress. Whenever the wind whipped her freshly shampooed hair across her eyes, she remembered the luscious curly hair on his chest.

The air smelled of life in all its glory. Roadside wildflowers filled the highway with their heady scent. The moon topped redbuds and dogwoods in full bloom.

Spring was right in the middle of resurrecting flora and feeling, while Joni and

Chance were completing a cycle begun by their grandfathers. Once he hit pay dirt, he'd pack up and leave. She knew that as well as she knew her own name. And she wondered what sort of winter would follow on the heels of his departure.

"We must be getting close," Chance said, his thigh muscles rippling under his jeans as he began applying the brakes. "I hear music."

Joni heard it too. She forced herself to ignore his leg rubbing against hers and looked straight ahead. "It's just around the bend. Turn left at the service road and follow it until you get to the circle of headlights."

Back when cattle was king and railroad was queen, the crossroads had been an important link to the outside world. Ranchers had come from miles around, bringing their livestock to be loaded and shipped all over the country. The low three-toned wail of the train whistle had carried the guarantee of prime beef raised by hardworking individuals rather than heartless corporations.

Nowadays, the crossroads sat empty and useless, abandoned in the name of progress. Cattle trucks and tankers did their *yeeowwing* on concrete instead of on cracked asphalt. Tourists bypassed dust bowl museums in favor of Disneyland, and even the farmers found it more convenient to use the highway.

But every Saturday night, weather permitting, everybody and his uncle gathered at the crossroads, circling their pickups as their pioneer ancestors had circled their wagons. Campfires had given way to headlights and fiddles to truck radios, but the people still did their dancing under the stars.

Chance drove around in search of a parking place, finally finding one between a rebuilt El Camino and a rusting Ford Ranchero. "For a county that's in the throes of a depression, they sure turn out a happy-go-lucky crowd."

Joni experienced a flash of regret when he released her to cut the engine, a reaction she quickly quelled. Needing the space, she slid back over to the passenger side. "It's fun and it's free."

"What more could a body want?" He left his headlights on and tuned his radio to the same country music station that everyone else was tuned to.

"A hairbrush," she remarked wryly, trying to fingercomb her hopelessly wind-tangled hair.

"In the glove compartment," he directed her, fiddling with the volume knob on the dashboard.

"Thanks, but…" She wasn't too keen on the idea of using someone else's hairbrush.

"Don't worry," he said perceptively, "it's yours."

She glanced at his dark profile against the glow of the other headlights. "Mine?"

"When I was helping Grandpa in the downstairs bathroom, I saw it sitting on the shelf." He sat back and gave her that lazy grin that never failed to jump-start her heart. "I figured you'd refuse the scarf, so while Diamond Jim Brady was stacking the deck, I stuck your hairbrush in the glove compartment."

"I see." She pasted on a bright smile and got her brush out, but the thought of him handling her personal things made her insides feel like taffy melting in the sun.

"Here." Chance reached over and took the hairbrush from her unresisting fingers. "Let me."

Joni started to refuse, but the firm set of his jaw told her that he would brook no argument. She presented him her back, her pulses thrumming in time to the three-chord country song rising and falling and filling the night.

One long, slow stroke and she knew she was lost. He seemed to know it, too, as he brought the brush back up to the crown of her head and pulled it down with enough pressure to disentangle the heavy, snarled strands but not enough to cause her pain.

She'd never realized such a simple act could also be so stimulating. He touched her nowhere else, yet she felt the repeated tug of the bristles from the top of her head to the tips of her toes.

"You have beautiful hair." He lifted it and sifted it through his fingers, letting it fall back to her narrow shoulders like spun cinnabar.

She nodded her thanks, not trusting her voice. He set the brush on the dashboard and took hold of her upper arm. "Turn around."

Against her better judgment she turned.

The music on the radio picked up a beat, as did her heart when his fingers captured her jaw.

"No, Chance." She raised her hands to his shoulders, wanting both to push him away and pull him closer.

"Yes, Joni." He kissed each corner of her lips and then traced the trembling line between them with the tip of his tongue.

She shut down her mind and parted her lips, surrendering to the power and the persuasion of a desire that had been too long denied. He matched his mouth to hers, a perfect fit, and seared her soul with a tongue of fire.

The ashes of emotion that she'd given up for dead flared to life, and she gloried in the blaze. But when the kiss ended and they drew apart, she knew it couldn't happen again without her getting badly burned.

Chance dropped his thumb and middle finger to the pulse points just below her jaw, circling them slowly, as if magnetizing her blood to follow the movements of his hand. "I've been wanting to do that since the day you came to the drilling site."

Joni pulled back in a panic, her hands clutching his, stopping those clever fingers before they robbed her of the will to resist. "Don't."

"Don't what?" he asked gently.

She released his hands and scrambled back to the passenger side. "Don't give me something to regret when you're gone."

He reached to bring her back. "How about something to remember?"

"I remember too much as it is." Her softly worded reply stilled him as effectively as a siren's blast.

A somebody-done-somebody-wrong song

came over the radio as Chance retracted his hand and studied her, huddled miserably against her door. He understood then. That bastard she'd been married to had a long reach.

Swearing roughly, he got out of the convertible and cut around to open her door. "Get out."

It cost Joni a great deal of courage to meet his eyes, but meet them she did. "You have every right to be angry—"

"You're damn right I do." He slammed her door so hard, it rocked the car on impact.

"If you'd rather I find another ride—"

"I brought you; I'll take you home."

Guiltily, she glanced away. "Please believe me, I didn't mean to lead you on."

"Not consciously, perhaps." He looked at her left hand, now clenched in a fist, fighting the urge to yank the ring off her finger and free her from the past. "But subconsciously, you wanted me to make love to you."

Joni jerked her head up in shock, but kept her voice down so the dancers wouldn't overhear. "That's a lie!"

"Is it?" Chance lowered his face close to her. "Then why did you get all dolled up tonight? And why were you practically sitting in my lap—"

"You're the one who insisted I sit there."

"You sure as hell didn't argue about it."

It all sounded so damnably true that she felt sick to her stomach, but still, she scoffed. "You're crazy."

He swore beneath his breath. "I'm crazy, all right. Crazy for wanting a woman who's married to a friggin' ghost."

Joni reeled as if he'd slapped her. Before she could respond, he spun on his heel and started toward the circle of headlights. Acting purely on instinct, she ran after him and grabbed his arm. "Where are you going?"

Chance paused only long enough to shake off her frantic hand. "Since there aren't any cold showers out here, I'm going to find a cold beer."

~ ~ ~

Loretta West was dressed to the cleavage in a slingshot of white sundress that played up her palomino paleness. Now, sitting in one of the folding chairs at the edge of the circle, she nudged Joni with her elbow. "Sweet Mother Macree, but your wildcatter sure is smooth."

Joni glanced at Chance, dancing with a

brunette in red Wranglers and boots, then back at Loretta. "For the last time, he's not my wildcatter."

"If you'd seen the daggers he was throwing at Simp Creed when you two were dancing a little while ago," Loretta said, you'd know why I keep calling him 'your' wildcatter."

"That's ridiculous," Joni sputtered. "Simp and I are friends—nothing more and nothing less."

"I know that and you know that," the buxom blonde agreed. "But if looks could kill, poor old Simp would be flat on the pavement right now."

Joni's startled gaze swung back to the circle, where Chance was guiding his partner around with skilled finesse. He caught her eye and nodded, then spun away, leaving her to stare at his broad shoulders and the brunette's familiar arm spanning them.

He danced the way he did everything else—with an easy rhythm rare in a man his size—and her heart tripped the light fantastic when she remembered his talented mouth. She twisted the plain gold band on her finger, trying to recall the cadence of Larry's kisses. But her memory rested on the sensual tempo of Chance's tongue, and she knew there was no dislodging it.

Loretta leaned over and laid her hand on Joni's. "The way you're worrying that ring, a body would think it was a ball and chain."

"I've thought about taking it off," Joni admitted softly, conscious of how heavy it had become these last two weeks. "But I've worn it for seven years now, and going without it would be like...going naked."

Loretta gave a throaty chuckle. "That's not a bad way to go."

Joni snatched her hand away. "Forget I even said anything, okay?"

The blonde sat back, not the least bit offended, and stared at her with disconcertingly candid blue eyes. "I see you've finally decided to let your hair down."

"Only for tonight."

"One small step in the right direction."

Joni looked around the circle, not liking the drift of the conversation, but she'd lost Chance in the crowd. "Did I tell you that Grandpa is taking some new medicine?"

"There he is."

"Who?" But her casual response didn't fool Loretta.

"Your wildcatter."

Joni felt a spurt of jealousy when she saw Chance laughing at something the brunette was saying. "I told you—"

"'He's not my wildcatter,'" Loretta finished for her.

The music ended then, and the dancers milled about the circle while commercials for everything from herbicide to hairspray jammed the airwaves.

Chance broke away from the brunette and headed for the community beer keg, where a woman in a billowy blue dress gave him the glad eye.

His words came back to haunt Joni. As much as she hated to admit it, he was right on target. But how did she go about divorcing herself from a ghost, not to mention the guilt?

The dulcet-voiced deejay announced the final number before he signed off for the night. It was a romantic ballad, one of Joni's favorites.

"Last dance is ladies' choice," Loretta reminded her.

"If he'd wanted to dance with me, he would have asked me," Joni answered stiffly.

Loretta had never married, but what she didn't know about men wasn't worth knowing. "Maybe he's waiting for you to make up your mind."

Joni looked as if she'd just swallowed one of the June bugs attracted by the headlights. "You saw us in the car?"

"And out of it."

The music started, casting a magic spell over the circle, and Joni realized she'd come to a crossroads of her own. She had to risk caring again.

She stood, her mind made up. "Thanks, Loretta."

The blonde winked a lacy eyelid. "Go get him, tiger."

Joni plunged into the crowd, dodging a dangerous elbow here and skirting a passionately embracing couple there.

Chance saw her working her way across the circle and met her in the middle. "I thought you'd never ask."

Her heart did a two-step when he put his arms around her. "Don't play so hard to get."

"Where you're concerned," he said as he molded her body to his, "I'm as easy as they come."

The beat surrounded them and permeated them, and starlight served as their personal strobe.

Joni danced with her eyes closed and her cheek against his chest, lost in the very life of him. She felt his hard thighs and warm hands. Heard the strong drum of his heart. Drank in the clean, woodsy smell of him. And she knew she was in the right place.

Their steps grew smaller as they drew closer. Joni wrapped her arms tightly around his neck, holding him as if she'd never let him go. Chance caressed her lower back, sensitizing her to his touch and spreading a slow, honeyed heat through the thin voile of her dress.

She whispered his name when his mouth brushed her temple, and they sealed their exquisite awareness of each other with a kiss that didn't end with the music.

"Good nights" and "good-byes" filled the air. Motors coughed to life. Bright yellow headlights turned into tiny red taillights. Silence fell as softly as a lover's sigh, but the moon and the stars held back the night.

Joni and Chance stood alone at the crossroads, each of them wondering where they went from there.

She knew he wanted to take her to bed.

He realized she wasn't ready yet.

But if one or the other of them didn't say or do something to break the spell that held them in thrall, bed was exactly where they were going to wind up.

The wind sang in the tall grass and the trees as Chance slipped his arm around Joni's reed of a waist and steered her toward the red convertible, saying softly, "Let's go home."

~ ~ ~

"Oh, no!" Guilt punched Joni in the stomach when she saw Dr. Rayburn's car parked in front of the house. "Something happened to Grandpa while we were gone."

She flung Chance's arm off her shoulder and slid over to the passenger side of the convertible. Before he could even brake to a complete stop, she opened her door and hit the ground at a run.

Pieces of gravel became embedded in her sandals and her toes, nicking her skin unmercifully as she tore across the driveway. Tears of frustration, not pain, filled her eyes when she tripped while going up the porch steps.

"Here." Chance came up beside her and grabbed hold of her arm, which kept her from falling flat on her face.

"Leave me alone." Joni swatted at his supporting hand almost hysterically.

"Dammit, I'm trying to help!"

"Haven't you done enough?"

Before he could ask her what she meant by that, she pulled out of his grasp and stumbled unaided up the remaining porch steps.

Dr. Rayburn opened the screen door for her.

"How's Grandpa?" she demanded.

"He's going to be fine." With his chaotic mop of hair, walrus mustache and rumpled white suit, Dr. Rayburn reminded Joni of Mark Twain.

"Thank God." Her legs went limp with relief, and this time she was grateful for Chance's hand at her elbow. "What happened, anyway?"

Dr. Rayburn pursed his lips. "Near as I can figure, Bat got to coughing so hard he couldn't catch his breath." He looked at Chance. "When your young roughneck called me, he sounded pretty shook up, so I said I'd come over and give him a shot to help him sleep."

"Where is Skinny?" Chance asked.

"I sent him home," the physician answered.

Confusion pinched Joni's small features. "How did he know to call you?"

"I left his number by the telephone," Chance said.

She bowed her head, ashamed that she hadn't thought of that herself, and whispered a heartfelt, "Thank you."

"How about a cup of coffee?" Chance offered.

Dr. Rayburn nodded. "Coffee sounds great."

In the kitchen Joni made the coffee and Chance cut three squares of her homemade gingerbread, topping them with fresh whipped cream. She refused to let herself think about how right it felt to be working side by side with him.

When he'd finished his late-night snack, Dr. Rayburn wrote out two new prescriptions for Grandpa. "I'm going to lower the dosage on his prednisone, which seems to be keeping him awake, and give him some sleeping pills to help him relax at the end of the day."

Chance pocketed the prescriptions. When Joni opened her mouth in protest, he shrugged and said, "I have to pick up some casing in town on Monday anyway, so I might as well get them filled while I'm there."

"I'll write you a check for whatever it costs." She realized she would be reimbursing him with his own money, but she wasn't about to accept his charity.

"Speaking of casing..." Dr. Rayburn eyed Chance over the rim of his coffee cup. "Bat tells me you'll be ready to start drilling next week."

"Good Lord willing and the creek don't rise," Chance confirmed.

The physician smiled at Joni. "What are

you going to do with all that money when your oil well comes in?"

She grinned. "Pay you."

He set his empty cup in the saucer, his expression turning serious. "I told you last month that I was willing to settle for what Medicare pays."

"That's not enough." She rued the day they'd had to drop their health insurance, but like most rural families, they simply couldn't afford the premiums.

He shook his shaggy head. "There's no Brink's trucks in funeral processions."

Chance reached for Dr. Rayburn's cup. "Would you like some more coffee?"

"No thanks," he declined. "Two's my limit this time of night."

Joni glanced at the cuckoo clock over the stove, surprised to see that it was nearly midnight. "Gosh, I didn't realize it was so late."

"Time flies when you're having fun," Chance quipped.

"Anything special happen out at the crossroads tonight?" Dr. Rayburn asked casually.

Her startled eyes met his wise ones. "What do you mean by special?"

"Oh..." He tugged thoughtfully at his

mustache. "You know, did anybody start a fight or kiss and make up? Did anybody fall in or out of love? The usual kind of special."

"Can't think of a thing," she said, and felt a twinge at the evasion.

The kitchen clock cuckooed, its timing perfect. Joni yawned and stretched. "I'm afraid it's way past my bedtime."

"Mine too." Dr. Rayburn brushed ginger-bread crumbs off the front of his wrinkled white suit onto the table. "I'm glad to see you're starting to get out among 'em again."

"Starting and stopping in one fell swoop," she stated emphatically.

"Your being here wouldn't have prevented Bat's spell," the physician said.

"I know, but—" She looked away, a cauldron of guilt and rage suddenly roiling inside her.

Dr. Rayburn leaned over and gave her a perceptive pat on the shoulder. "It wouldn't have prevented that either."

She put a lid on her emotions and stood. "We'll never know for sure, will we?"

Mustache fluttering, the physician followed suit. "I guess not."

Chance hadn't said a word during this last exchange. But on seeing that closed expression on Joni's face—an expression he'd become all too familiar with these past two weeks—he decided to find out what the hell was behind it.

Toward that end, he got to his feet and picked up the doctor's black leather bag. "I need to put the top up on my car, so I'll see the doctor out."

"Fine." Joni stacked their few dishes and carried them to the sink.

"Your grandpa should sleep all night with no problem after that shot I gave him," Dr. Rayburn said in parting.

Joni made short work of the dishes, then went to the dining room to check on Grandpa before going upstairs to bed herself.

One set of shutters was folded back, and a lump the size of an egg lodged in her throat as she studied his sleeping face in the moonlight. His cheeks were sunken, and the skin that stretched across the bones seemed transparent. But the meter of his breathing, if not entirely normal, was relaxed.

His dog, a bluetick hound he'd named Sooner because it would "sooner chase rabbits than stay home," lay curled at his side. It raised alert eyes to her now, as if to assure her that it would stay put while she slept.

She reached across Grandpa's peaceful form to cup the bluetick's trusty muzzle in a caress, then turned and ran from the room before she lost it completely.

Upstairs, she washed her face and brushed her teeth in record time, not wanting to risk a confrontation with Chance. She'd been on an emotional elevator ever since she'd met him, and she really wasn't up to answering any of the questions she'd seen in his eyes when he'd left the kitchen.

Turning away from the bathroom mirror to keep from being devoured by the hunger in her own eyes, she beat a hasty retreat to her bedroom. She undressed in the dark, then lay alone in her double bed as she had a thousand nights before.

But sleep didn't come with its usual ease. The soft wind wafting through her screen seemed to whisper his name. Chance... Chance...Chance. And the memory of his strong arms and sensual mouth awakened needs in her that no amount of tossing and turning could exhaust.

Deeply pitched masculine voices rode a windflaw. Car doors slammed. The convertible top purred up, and Dr. Rayburn's tires crunched down the gravel driveway. But she waited in vain for the opening squeak and closing slap of the screen door and the steady thud of boot steps coming up the stairs.

Finally, overcome by curiosity about what could be keeping Chance, she flung herself out of her inhospitable bed and went to the window. She knelt and crossed her arms on the sill, watching him, unseen, as he paced the driveway, smoking.

Moonlight poured over him like cream from a pitcher, running down those broad shoulders and that marvelously symmetrical back. The rolled-up sleeves of his white shirt contrasted starkly with his dusky skin.

He took a deep drag on his cigarette, then dropped it and crushed it underfoot. Much as a lover's fingers would, the wind mussed his thick hair. She fought a madcap urge to run down the stairs and out the door and rumple it properly.

Muttering obscene curses that would have given a mule skinner cause for pause, he continued to pace. Once, he stopped and looked long and hard up at her darkened window. She dodged sideways, horrified to realize he might have caught her spying on him. But the instant she heard the regular crunch of gravel under his impatient feet, she went back to her post.

Joni took no comfort in knowing that he felt as restless as she did. For him, this was just a detour on the road to satisfaction. But for her, it was as devastating as a head-on collision.

She didn't move again until he turned to come inside. Then she hurried back to bed before the creaky old floorboards could betray her. Lying there in the dark, her body tense as a bow, she listened to the muffled bang of the screen door and the mounting thump of his boot steps.

A sigh of relief tinged with regret escaped her lips when she heard his bedroom door click closed. She told herself that the nights were always the hardest, but it seemed they were harder than ever now that Chance was living under the same roof.

Chapter 6

Joni tossed and turned. And she dreamed...

The barn doors were open.

Impatience surged inside her as she parked the pickup and climbed out.

The wind caught the doors and slammed them against the side of the barn.

Damn Larry's hide, anyway! She knew he'd been depressed lately about their financial situation, but that didn't excuse his carelessness. Yanking off the hairnet she wore for her waitressing job, she started across the farmyard on aching feet that had just finished a double shift. Did she have to do everything around here?

The doors swung wildly, eluding her grasp.

She struggled with one door, pushing it closed with her weight, but the other one creaked elusively. Grandpa was in no shape to oil the hinges, and Larry just ignored the horrible noise they made. She'd just have to do it herself.

The light in the tack room was on.

"Larry?"

The echo of her own voice in the vastness

was her only response.

Feeling a vague premonition, she walked past the now empty milking stalls toward the tack room.

The banshee wail of the wind, the squeak of the hinges, the crash of the barn door behind her caused the hair an the back of her neck to stand on end.

Long afterward, she would remember the dim light spilling from his private little domain, the metallic taste of fear in her mouth as she approached it. "If this is your idea of a joke, Larry Fletcher—"

The foreclosure notice lay on his tool bench.

She picked it up with shaking hands, wishing she'd been at home when the mail came. But when one of the other waitresses had called in sick, she'd jumped at the chance to work a double shift.

The barn door screaked open; the wind cried mournfully, nature's keening; the rafters shivered in reply.

A terrible cold embraced her as she pocketed the notice and reached for the oil can. What she saw when she turned to leave the tack room froze her in her tracks.

The boots, cracked and worn.

The body, collapsed in the corner.

The...

~ ~ ~

There, he heard it again.

A muffled scream.

Chance extinguished his half-smoked cigarette in the ashtray on the nightstand and swung his naked legs over the edge of the bed. Stepping into his discarded jeans, he fastened them on the run.

He'd been lying there wide awake, mulling over the horror story that Dr. Rayburn had told him, when he'd heard the first scream.

Silence had followed.

And then another scream.

The hall was dark as lampblack.

He opened the door to Joni's room.

Moonlight spilled through the lace-curtained windows and across a wicker confection of a bed that seemed totally out of keeping with the rest of the sparsely furnished house.

She had her back to him, her face buried in her pillow. The sheets, as lavishly trimmed as a Victorian petticoat, were tangled about her legs. Her narrow shoulders shook in the grip of nocturnal terror.

Chance didn't even hesitate. Didn't stop to think that what he was about to do could upset the tenuous balance that already existed between them. He simply broad-jumped across the room, onto the bed, and gathered her into his arms, rocking her and holding her tight against him.

"Larry?"

Chance winced when she grabbed frantic handfuls of his chest hair. But in all honesty, he welcomed the physical pain. It helped him forget the emotional sting of being called by that S.O.B.'s name.

"Oh, God, I dreamed you—"

"Hush, darlin'." Chance combed soothing fingers through her sweat-damp hair, rubbed his chin on the top of her head, ran his hands down her delicate back. "I'm here."

The wind luffed the curtains, Quaker lace tied back with matching wisps of material.

She relaxed her grip on his chest hair and curled up against him like a kitten looking for a warm lap. "I'm cold."

Chance propped his bare back against the curlicued headboard and held her in a close embrace. Desire knifed through him when she draped her leg over his, crooked it so that her knee practically nudged the fly on his jeans.

"The hinges on the barn door need oiling," she mumbled.

His mouth curved in a smile. She was

starting to sound like her old self again. "I'll do it first thing in the morning."

"That's what you said yester—" Sleep, peaceful sleep, claimed her in midsentence.

Chance did his damnedest to relax, but his body felt nervier than a bad tooth. Her soft hair feathered his lips and her steady breathing tickled his nipples. A small, firm breast rode the swell of his rib cage, while a slender hand branded his stomach just above the beltline of his jeans.

Think about something else, he admonished himself when her knee slid up a smidgen and her hand slipped lower. Anything else!

A silver-dollar moon beamed through the picture frame of a window, highlighting the summerhouse nostalgia that reigned supreme in her private retreat.

Serrated tendrils of Boston fern grew lush and long atop a tiered stand. The screen guarding the far corner was a veritable fantasy of hearts and spit curls. A snooze-inducing chaise sat at the foot of the plumply pillowed bed.

First the old-fashioned dress, and now the white wicker room. Who'd have ever dreamed this practical little package in his arms had a hidden romantic streak?

He ground his head against the head-board when her aristocratic nose grazed his highly sensitive nipple. At this rate, he'd never get to sleep!

But sometime before dawn, Chance finally slept. As his eyes drifted closed, it occurred to him that this was the first time in his life he'd gone to bed with a woman with no thought of making love to her before the night was over.

~ ~ ~

For a woman who was used to sleeping alone, the musky smell of a male first thing in the morning proved to be a real eye-opener. As did the hair-rough chest that pillowed her cheek.

Joni tried to remember the sequence of events that had led to her compromising position with Chance, but she drew a blank. Lying perfectly still otherwise, she glanced at the digital clock on her nightstand.

It was time to get up.

Past time, she corrected herself with a start when she raised her knee a mite and realized she'd awakened with a fully aroused man.

Rolling her head back ever so carefully,

she let her eyes wander up his tanned throat to the proud chin. His lips promised humor and hinted at passion—both its savage fury and its splendid fire. That nose had been on the receiving end of a fist at least once, and she hated to think what the other guy must've looked like when the fight was over.

She gasped softly when she lifted her eyes to his and found them steadily watching her.

"Good morning, sunshine." His sleep-and-smoke husky voice reverberated in her ear.

"What are you doing here?" she whispered.

"You don't remember?"

"No."

"You had a nightmare."

It came back to her then in a chilling rush. The boots, the body, the—She swallowed convulsively and raised her head. "Thank you."

He was intrigued to see that her skin was so tender, it retained the crinkly impression of his chest hair. "My pleasure."

She straightened her leg and, ever so gingerly, lifted it off him. "You can let go of me now.

His possessive hand warmed the valley of her waist. "I kinda like it like this."

Vexed because she did, too, she pulled

free of his hold and flounced over onto her back. "I need to get dressed."

He settled in for the duration, looking more masculine than ever in her bridal-white bed. "I'm not stopping you."

"Chance—"

"You called me Larry in your sleep."

Joni detected a slight edge to his voice. "A natural mistake, under the circumstances."

"Maybe so," he agreed with exaggerated casualness. "But I think at least a part of you knew all along that it was me who was holding you."

She rolled away from him, the galling truth she'd been groping toward in the dark of night suddenly tumbling into place in the clear light of his statement. To put it bluntly, she *had* known it was Chance and not Larry who'd come to her rescue.

Not the whole time—he was wrong about that. At first she'd been drowning in a deathly sea and seeking a lifeline. But gradually she'd begun to realize that the man who was holding her, comforting her, was the same man she'd sworn to avoid at all costs.

Instead of pushing him away, as she should have, she'd wrapped herself around him like a sweet potato vine. A slow heat stole over her as she recalled the chafe of denim against her bare legs and the insides of her thighs, the crimp of hair beneath her cheek. That much she vividly remembered.

And her dreams...Toward daybreak they'd taken such a sensual turn, it made her wonder if she'd only been dreaming.

"What was the nightmare about?" Chance thought it would be good for her to talk about it, to get it off her chest.

Joni snapped back to the here and now. She sat up, sickened and ashamed, and shook her head. "I don't want to discuss it."

He wondered who she was trying to protect—herself or that bastard who'd been her husband. Stretching an arm across the bed, he reached to bring her back to his side. "You can't keep it bottled up inside you forever, you know."

"Don't touch me!" Guilt propelled her to her feet. She rounded on him, hands on hips and blue eyes flashing the same defiance that had kept her going when all else had failed. "You weaseled your way into my house. Into my bed, even! But you're not—repeat, not— going to weasel your way into my—"

She cut her sentence off, realizing suddenly that he could see through her thin nightgown. Worse yet, he didn't even have the decency to pretend otherwise!

Dropping her arms to her sides, Joni spun away from those jade green eyes and stalked to her chest of drawers. Turnabout was fair play.

Chance had watched countless women undress in his day. Hell, he'd even helped on occasion! But for sheer eroticism, none of the stripteases he'd witnessed could hold a candle to the sight of this nettled female getting dressed underneath her nightgown.

His pulse went freewheeling when she bent down to step into clean white hipsters, displaying a tulip flare of bottom. Then she drove him into a fine madness by pulling them up over those long-stemmed legs with a provocative lack of haste.

Both her arms and her bra disappeared inside the gown then. He had to smile at the way her elbows gouged at their cotton confines as she fumbled with the front clasp. But he gulped air, huffed it out when, on reaching for the rest of her clothes, sunlight silhouetted pert breasts encased in lace.

She made a big production of getting into her jeans and checking over her shoulder to be sure they didn't cup her derriere too tightly. Whether she realized it or not, they revealed more feminine assets than they hid.

Chance, his stony jaw shadowed by a night's growth of beard, met her eyes in the mirror. It did him good to see her blush, to know she'd trapped herself in the same sensuous web in which she'd ensnared him.

Quickly averting her gaze, she donned a sleeveless blouse and buttoned it with clumsy fingers. That done, she pulled the gown over her head and her hair from beneath her shirt collar.

"That was quite a show," he said sarcastically.

Joni refused to look at him as she folded her nightgown and put it in the bottom drawer. She'd started out wanting revenge, but she'd ended up wanting him.

He slid off the bed and approached her from behind, and she knew she was in for it. "What do you do for an encore—climb into your widow's weeds?"

Confession quivered on the tip of her tongue. She wanted to turn and tell him that she'd outsmarted herself with that stupid stunt, that she was hurting, too, but humiliation had her by the throat.

"There's a word for women like you..."

She burned crimson as he pressed his hard male shape against the soft curves of her bottom, the heat of him scorching her

through the bite of zipper and the dual bar-
riers of denim.

"Women who lead a man on and then
leave him—"

"Get out of my room!" she flared when
she found her voice.

He stood motionless for a moment, as
though daring her to repeat her demand.
Then the regrets he'd held at bay all night
claimed her with renewed force as he spun
and stamped toward the door.

When he slammed it shut behind her, she
rubbed her throbbing temples and sighed
wearily, "Get out of my dreams."

Chapter 7

Drilling started at sunup on Tuesday.

Chance gave the signal with a gloved hand. The motor rumbled to life, the roughnecks went to work, and all systems were go.

Standing on the rig floor, he almost laughed out loud to feel the great structure quivering under the powerful drive necessary to spin a quarter-mile of steel pipe on end.

God bless America, but he loved the oil business! It wasn't the money that motivated him as much as it was the challenge, the gamble, and the flirtation with his old flame—danger.

Most people called him reckless. But those were the same people who'd never taken a piece of fallow ground and proven it productive. Nor had they risked everything they owned on the wheel of fortune and come out a winner. More's the pity, they didn't know what they were made of because they'd yet to tread the razor's edge and walk away whole.

So let 'em sit on their safe little sidelines and gossip their fool heads off. No skin off his nose. He knew what he was and he knew what he wanted.

He wanted black gold from the earth's belly. Wanted to stand back and watch it gush skyhigh, blocking out the sun. Then he wanted to lay his grandfather's memory to rest for eternity.

Even more than that, he wanted to see Joni's red, red hair spread across his pillow. Wanted to kiss her till his life's breath flowed through her lungs and into her blood system. Bury himself so deep inside her, he could feel her heart beating. Make her body a part of his and his a part of hers.

It was the damnedest thing, the way she kept popping into his head when he least expected it.

He'd had his share of casual affairs. No strings attached on either side and no tears when it was time for him to move on. But he'd never met a woman who'd fought him tooth-and-nail and kept him coming back for more.

Until Joni.

Beat the hell out of him. He'd had money to burn, women to spare and cars running out the ying-yang. On the whole, he hadn't done too badly. Lately, though, he'd been aware of some visceral lack, some vital element that was missing from his life.

Truth was, he wanted Joni so much it hurt. But *hurt* was the operative word here.

She'd suffered enough. More than enough, if Dr. Rayburn's story and her nightmare were anything to go by. He'd seen the once-burned-twice-shy expression on her face, felt her trembling in his arms. And he couldn't—he wouldn't—trifle with her tender emotions.

Couldn't tell her that he loved her when he wasn't even sure what the word meant. Wouldn't promise her that he'd settle down when he had drilling obligations from one end of the state to the other.

Because—hell, he didn't know why. But he knew he didn't want to hurt her—ever. Didn't want those gorgeous blue eyes on his conscience when it was time for him to go.

So he denied his desire for her and got on with the business of drilling for oil, blissfully ignorant of the fact that the initial test of true love is putting the other person first.

~ ~ ~

The first day of summer and her tomato plants were already three feet tall. Just went to show what a person could accomplish when she put her mind to it.

Joni placed a gloved hand on the small of

her aching back and straightened up from her uncomfortable weeding position. At the rate they were growing, she'd have ripe tomatoes by the Fourth of July.

That's not all she'd have, either.

Finished weeding, she took off her work gloves and shaded her eyes with a hand that had shown remarkable improvement since she'd begun wearing them on a daily basis. She looked over her raised tomato beds and out toward the cornfield, where the drilling rig rose like a phoenix from the ashes of despair.

A slender spire of steel gossamer that towered above her thrifty farm, it seemed as incongruous as a tree growing in mid-ocean. No workers were visible at the moment, but the steady clatter and rumble coming from the derrick told her that drilling was proceeding right on schedule.

Two weeks from start to strike, barring equipment breakdowns, Chance had said before he'd left to pick up that load of casing and Grandpa's prescriptions yesterday. But it was what he hadn't said that gnawed at her now. He'd yet to mention either her nightmare or her foolish behavior the following morning.

Her temper had a terribly short fuse.

Sometimes that worked to her advantage. Back her into a corner and she'd fight like a tiger to get out. Other times she was her own worst enemy. Give her enough rope and she'd hang herself.

She still cringed when she remembered her reverse striptease. Chance had provoked her, pure and simple. But two wrongs didn't make a right, and on meeting his eyes in the mirror, she'd realized she was as much to blame for the incident as he was.

The rig swayed under the force of the wind, reminding her that all was not lost. Dropping her hand, she started toward the house and her never-ending bookwork, wondering which of their creditors to pay and which she could put off for another month. At least she wouldn't have to worry about that much longer.

Come July, she'd have oil. Barrels of it. And money. Piles of it. But she wouldn't have Chance. Couldn't have Chance. He wasn't the settling kind. Wasn't a man she could depend on when the chips were down. And that broke her heart because, fool that she was, she loved him.

She loved him!

Loved the rowdy streak of laughter that ran through him. The inner strength and rugged individualism that radiated from him. She even loved the trace of chauvinism that surfaced in him every so often, though a little of it certainly went a long way.

She loved him so much, she wanted to shout it to the world. But she couldn't tell a soul—not even Grandpa—because she loved him too much not to let him go.

~ ~ ~

"Grandpa?"

"Out here."

Joni stepped to the front screen door and peered out. A ragged patch of cloud had eclipsed the moon, and she could barely make out her grandfather's shape, hunched forward in the old oak porch swing.

It just tore her up to see him sitting alone in the darkness, struggling to breathe. But the prednisone that eased his cough kept him awake, and he refused to take the sleeping pills that Dr. Rayburn had prescribed. Claimed they made him sleepy at all the wrong times.

"Mind if I join you?" Joni asked.

"Don't stay up on my account," Grandpa protested.

"It's a little early for bed yet—even for

me." She slipped out the door and started across the porch. The wind had died down to an occasional whiff, and only a trace of dust lingered in the air.

He patted the seat beside him and moved over some, smiling when she took her place. That bit of exertion cost him dearly. He hunched forward again, his breath coming short and hard.

Joni's heart and hand went out to him as she reached over and gently rubbed his back. Her eyes brimmed with grief when her palm contoured the emaciated ridges of spinal column and shoulder blade that protruded beneath his flannel shirt.

"Damnation!" Trying his best not to cough—it hurt so bad—Grandpa shook his head in self-disgust. "I'd shoot a horse that sounded like this."

Her hand stilled; her heart dove into a tailspin. "That's a terrible thing to say!"

"It's true, though," he said philosophically. "We treat animals more humanely than we do people."

She hid her anguish behind anger, an automatic defense with her. "I'm warning you, Grandpa, if you don't stop talking like this, I'll call Dr. Rayburn and have you hospitalized."

"It's not the dying I'm afraid of." He panted with the effort of speaking. "It's the doctors."

"You can't give up." Not when they were so close to being able to afford a lung specialist. "I won't let you."

A spark of his old spirit flashed across his face. "A body's got a right to die."

Joni clamped her hands over her ears. "Stop it!"

Grandpa grabbed her wrists and forced her hands down, surprising her with his tenacity. "Promise me you won't send me to the hospital. Won't let them jam tubes up my nose and down my throat."

"Please—"

"Promise me you'll let me die at home."

Was this how she repaid the man who'd raised her single-handedly? By making a promise she wasn't sure she could keep?

A jumble of thoughts played tricks on Joni's mind, appearing and disappearing so fast, she couldn't really grasp them. Grandpa wiping her tears when she skinned her knees...Grandpa waiting up for her when she came home from her first date... Grandpa walking her down the aisle when she married Larry, up the aisle when she buried him.

She coughed to clear the rust from her throat. "I promise."

He released her hands. "Thank you, darlin'."

They swung silently then, listening to crickets and barn owls and the rhythmic pounding of the drill bit. Odd, how the *chirrups* and *screeches* and *thuds* all harmonized to create their own special symphony.

Drilling had been going on day and night for a week now, keeping Chance away from the house from sunup to sundown, and sometimes later than that.

Like tonight, for instance.

He'd called her from the trailer while she was fixing supper to tell them to go ahead and eat without him. She'd offered to run his plate over to the site, but he'd refused, saying he'd just grab a bite of whatever was in the refrigerator there. So supper had been a lonely affair.

The moon peeked through the clouds just then and Joni glanced toward the cornfield, her eyes seeking but not finding Chance's muscular figure. The towering derrick had melted into the night. In its place were groups of ruby lights—airplane warnings—high up against a sky of blue-black velvet.

On the rig floor fantastic shadows danced here and there as naked electric bulbs swung in the intermittent breeze. Stacks of pipe glinted in the moonlight, and wet drilling mud glistened on men and machinery.

A chain clinked musically and the diesel engine drummed softly. The sound of money in the making... The sound of good-bye.

Determined not to brood, Joni got to her feet and crossed to the porch railing, looking across the farmyard. A sense of life renewed blossomed in her smile when she located the raised beds where her tomatoes grew.

She kept her garden meticulously neat, watering and weeding as though her sanity depended on it. Perhaps it did. She knew she'd come dangerously near her own breaking point after Larry died, wondering and worrying about the future. Working till she dropped had given her an opportunity to let off some steam. More important, it had given her the order and symmetry she hadn't been able to impose on any other aspect of her life.

"Well," Grandpa said now, "I guess Chance isn't coming home tonight."

"I guess not." Joni realized he missed the wildcatter as much as she did and she told herself that they were going to have to get used to an empty house sooner or later. He'd be gone in no time flat.

Too agitated to stand there just doing nothing, she turned to help Grandpa out of the swing and into the house. "Come on, it's past your—" But the rest of her sentence rode a warm zephyr into the night when she saw Chance cutting across the cornfield. The moon broke completely through the clouds, lighting his path, and her heart did a welcome-home pirouette.

"Speak of the devil..." Joni wasn't sure if it was the rig or her pounding pulse that shook the porch where she stood when he took the steps two at a time.

"Howdy, stranger," Grandpa said with a grin.

"Are you hungry?" she asked.

"How's the drilling going?"

"Do you like cold fried chicken?"

"How about a game of pitch?"

Chance raised his callused palms, effectively putting a stop to their excited bombardment. "In reverse order, maybe later, love it, fine, and famished."

Joni and Grandpa fell silent as they fumbled to slot his answers into the proper questions.

"But first," he said before they'd quite succeeded, "I'm going to take a shower."

Mud covered his lean body from head to foot, but in Joni's eyes he'd never looked better. She smiled. "There's a whole stack of clean towels in the linen closet."

He flashed her that engaging grin before he turned to go inside. "Thanks."

Twenty minutes later the three of them sat on the porch just like a regular family at the end of the day, Joni and Grandpa in the swing and Chance in the wicker rocker with a plate on his lap.

He polished off three pieces of the golden brown chicken and two slices of homemade bread slathered with butter before he set his plate on the round table beside the rocker and gave a sigh of repletion. "That was really good."

A frown etched Joni's forehead. "Didn't you eat today?"

"Didn't have time." Chance lifted his beer bottle to his lips and took a long swig. He'd started keeping a six-pack in her refrigerator so he could have a cold one every night.

Funny, he thought as he drained the bottle and set it aside, before he met Joni he often knocked off a whole six-pack in a single sitting. But now he never wanted more than one.

"I told you when you called that I'd be glad to fix you a plate and run it over to the site," she reminded him.

"And I appreciated the offer," he replied. "But it wouldn't be fair to the other guys if I ate a square meal and they ate catch-as-catch-can."

Grandpa asked Chance a question about the drilling procedure, which prompted a discussion about the old "cable tool" method as opposed to the modem "rotary" method.

Joni didn't pay any mind to what the men were saying because she had a plan she was mulling over. If it worked out the way she hoped, they'd all get to spend a little more time together. And if it didn't...at least she would have given it her best shot.

She came out of her reverie only to realize that Chance had just asked Grandpa why he'd never drilled for oil before.

"I lost interest when I lost Ruthann," Grandpa answered quietly.

"You must have loved her very much."

"There's not a day goes by that I don't miss her with every fiber of my being."

Chance envied the old man his memories. He'd never felt that way about a woman. Never known that kind of love. That kind of loyalty. He wondered if he ever would.

Grandpa's eyes narrowed as he looked back through a fog of fifty-some years. "We had our differences, of course. She liked to do things on the spur of the moment. I liked to plan things down to the last little detail. She never met a stranger, while I was slower to warm up to people. But we had the basics in common."

Joni remembered what Chance had said about showing her what *they* had in common and wondered if he remembered it too.

He did.

Their eyes met in the moonlight.

"Both of us loved the land," Grandpa went on musingly. "And both of us welcomed the challenge it presented. More important yet, both of us were willing to *fight*—"

A coughing fit cut him off then.

Like a well-trained rescue team, Joni and Chance jumped to their feet and went to Grandpa's aid.

She gave him a sleeping pill.

He got him into his pajamas.

She folded back the covers and fluffed the pillows.

He carried him to bed and laid him gently in place.

She kissed that leathery old cheek.

He turned off the light.

The long-case clock in the hallway chimed ten times.

"I think I'll leave my bedroom door open, in case he wakes up." Her emotions flayed raw by the events of the past few hours, the last three years, Joni couldn't make direct eye contact with Chance for fear he'd see how much she needed him tonight.

He walked her to the bottom of the stairs and stopped, studying her bowed head. Knowing he could take her tonight. Knowing it would break her in the long run. Knowing he was doing the right thing when he turned away and left her to go up alone.

"Chance..." She called after him so chokily, it damn near did him in.

"Don't say it, Joni." Better the small hurt now than the big heartache later on, he told himself as he stalked to the screen door.

"Wh-where are you going?"

"Back to the drilling site."

"Will you be gone long?"

"A couple of hours at least."

She pressed her fist to her stomach. "I'll wait up."

He punched the screen door open with the heel of his hand and sent it crashing against the outside wall. "Don't bother."

"What's this?"

"Thirst aid."

Chance got up and came around from behind his desk, where he'd been working on the drilling log. He'd heard of first aid, of course, but...

"*Thirst* aid?"

"Iced tea and freshly squeezed lemonade." Joni set the small cooler she'd lugged from her truck into the trailer on the linoleum floor, which had been swept and scrubbed since the last time she's seen it.

He shook his dark head in confusion. "I still don't get it."

"Grandpa and I brought drinks and dinner to you and your crew." She knelt beside the cooler and removed the two plastic pitchers that held their liquid refreshment.

"You're kidding!" He put the containers she handed him on the dinette table, the surface of which bore not a single dirty ashtray or empty beer bottle. "Why would you do something like that?"

"It's not good for you to go all day without eating." She closed the cooler lid, then stood and opened the trailer door. "Come on, I've got a big pot of ham and beans and two pans of cornbread in the bed of my truck."

Grandpa had the dinner bell.

The roughnecks came running to see what all the commotion was about and went back to the rig a half hour later with their bellies full of Joni's good home cooking and their pockets lighter by a couple of quarters, thanks to Grandpa's deal.

"I can't believe you went to all this trouble," Chance said as he spooned the last bite of beans out of the cast iron pot that sat in the middle of the table.

Joni looked around her with something akin to awe. "That makes us even then, because I can't believe how you've cleaned up your trailer."

"Well, it still wouldn't pass the white-glove test."

The lines on either side of his mouth deepened in a mischievous smile. "But after someone called it a 'boar's nest'—"

"Don't remind me." She blushed. "It was none of my business and I shouldn't have criticized."

"Hey," he assured her sincerely, "I'm the first to admit it was a mess. You just spurred me on to doing something I should have done months ago."

"It looks nice."

"I'm glad you approve."

They stared at each other meaningfully.

So far neither one of them had said anything about last night. But now the silence fairly vibrated with the words they dared not verbalize.

I waited up until after midnight, sad blue eyes said.

I told you not to bother, somber green eyes answered.

The exchange lasted but several seconds before Grandpa asked, "Is this what I think it is?"

"What?" Their voices collided as their gazes swerved toward one of the easy chairs that had replaced the sagging sofa.

"This." Grandpa held up an old felt hat. Ribbon-less and battered, it looked like something even a hobo would have rejected.

"It was my grandfather's hat." Chance slid swarthy fingers up and down his tea glass, where condensation had made it slippery.

Joni watched his long, lean fingers stroking the glass, studied the shading of hair on his knuckles, and could just imagine...

"I thought so." Grandpa put the hat back on the smoking stand that separated the easy chairs. "I helped your mother chase it down the day he found our oil."

"He called it his 'witching hat.'" Chance wiped away a droplet of moisture with his thumb, and Joni noticed how clean his nails were.

"If I live to be a hundred, which I won't, I'll never forget the sight of him prancing around this field like a man possessed." The memory brought a sparkle to Grandpa's eyes.

"He showed me the steps one night when he was feeling no pain." Staring at the amber-colored tea that bore such a strong resemblance to the whiskey that had killed the oil witch, Chance smiled wryly. "I have to admit it looked pretty wild."

"You kept the hat as a memento?" Grandpa asked.

Chance laughed, but there was little humor in the sound. "For what it's worth, which isn't much."

Joni wondered what private pain seasoned his sarcastic comment, but she didn't feel it was her place to probe.

"How about a cook's tour of the site?" Chance asked then.

"I'd like that," she agreed.

"If you don't mind," Grandpa said around a yawn, "I think I'll skip the tour and take a little nap instead."

Chance stood. "There's some bunks in back if you want to stretch out."

Grandpa nodded. "That'd be great."

Joni put her pots and pans and pitchers in the cooler and set it by the front door while Chance got Grandpa settled down.

She had to laugh when she noticed that a new calendar from the People's Bank of Redemption had replaced the out-of-date pinup girl on the wall.

"What's so funny?" Chance asked when he came back.

"You," Joni answered with a firm smirk.

"Oh, yeah?" He crossed the trailer in two long strides that left him standing so close, she could see the tiny gold flecks in his green, green eyes. "What's so funny about me?"

"For one thing, I can't quite picture you down on your hands and knees scrubbing the floor."

He grimaced. "It wasn't a pretty sight."

"And for another, I can't imagine your putting out a welcome mat that says 'Wipe your feet or prepare to meet your Maker.'"

He grinned. "Desperate situations call for daring solutions."

They were whispering so as not to disturb Grandpa. But they needn't have bothered because the noise from the rig protected their privacy as securely as the walls and doors did.

"Have I thanked you yet for bringing dinner?" Chance placed his hands on either side of her waist.

"Not properly." Joni put hers on his broad shoulders, surprised by her own boldness.

Emerald eyes rayed into blue. "How could I thank you properly?"

Her sapphire gaze caught his fire and returned its radiance. "Well, you could write me a bread-and-butter note."

"That doesn't sound personal enough."

"Or you could send me some flowers."

"There isn't a florist within forty miles of here."

She tilted her head back. "Well, then you think of something."

He lowered his. "I already have."

Joni answered his descending mouth with her own escalating need. Her lips parted, all but begging to be possessed. Her body became a bundle of nerve endings, aching everywhere for his soothing touch.

Chance heeded her silent yearnings and melded their mouths together. His tongue pressed home, seeking and finding its counterpart. One of his hands slipped below her waist to cup her firm bottom. The other inched upward to the outer curve of her breast.

Sorrow was a thing of the past, parting a thing of the future, she thought as she threaded her fingers through his sable-thick hair and bound him to her for the time being.

Reality intruded with a crunch and a shudder, and the resulting silence was deafening.

Chance lifted his mouth from Joni's, muttering curses by the carload. Then he smiled a little crookedly, slipped an arm around her waist, and led her to the door. "Sounds like the cook's tour just turned into a fishing trip."

She went with him willingly. "What are we going fishing for?"

He stopped only long enough to plop a hard hat on each of their heads. "A broken drill pipe."

The grinding rumble of the diesel engine had ceased, but there was an air of bustle about the crew. They were getting ready to raise the upper end of the pipe so they could pull the lower part out of the hole and make repairs.

Joni had worn her oldest jeans and her waffle stompers, so she wasn't worried about getting muddy. She stood in a corner on the rig floor. But instead of feeling excluded, as she had the last time, she felt as if she really belonged.

Tex gave her the high sign, and Skinny fell all over his own feet when she thanked him for what he'd done for Grandpa. The other roughnecks nodded in passing.

Chance issued orders left and right, which everyone hustled to obey. When the upper part of the pipe had been raised, he screwed the fishing tool to the end of it.

The tool was a heavy metal cylinder of slightly greater diameter than the pipe. It looked like a giant lead pencil with a very long tapered point. Around the taper were closely cut teeth that gave it the appearance of a round file.

While the roughnecks watched the fishing operation, Joni watched Chance.

The brim of his hard hat threw his masculine features into dusky shadow, but the calm, serious line of his profile told her how much he loved his work. His arm muscles knotted under the sleeves of his T-shirt, and her eyes roved hungrily on down to his thighs, corded and strong as they strained against the fabric of his jeans.

He'd left his gloves in the trailer and was guiding the metal tool with his bare brown hands. She swallowed hard at the memory of his touch and turned away, trying to forget and failing miserably.

"I think I've got it." Chance said just then.

Joni turned back to him, and sure enough he was hauling the broken pipe out of the hole.

Skinny stood in awe of his skill. "I can't believe you snagged that sucker on the first try."

"That's because I've got better things to do than to fool around with this all day." Chance looked at Joni and smiled, his straight white teeth a brilliant contrast to his dark face. Then he turned the repair work over to Tex and started across the rig floor.

"Where were we when we were so rudely interrupted?" he asked, giving her a look of wicked amusement.

"As I recall," she answered, all innocence and light, "you were going to give me a cook's tour of the site."

His grin widened. "How about a bird's-eye view instead?"

She glanced at the nearby scaffold and shuddered. "No thanks."

"You're afraid of heights?" Remembering how she'd started to come after him that first day, he really was surprised.

"I get a nosebleed if I stand on a chair." she admitted. "I'm liable to have a hemor-rhage if I go up on a scaffold."

"You don't know what you're missing."

"A blood transfusion."

"I'm serious."

"So am I!"

Chance bent his knees, bringing his face down on a level with hers. "Do it for Grandpa."

"Now you're playing dirty pool." She knew that Grandpa would give his right arm for an opportunity to go up on the rig.

His grin was as good as an admission of guilt.

She looked at him, her blue eyes enormous under the brim of the hard hat. "I'll go up on two conditions."

"Name 'em."

"First, you have to wear your safety line."

"Are you afraid I'll fall?"

She lifted her chin a notch. "Yes."

He nodded decisively. "I'll do it."

"And second, we go only as far as the first platform."

"I'll tell Skinny to start the engine."

Before she could say another word, Joni found herself wearing a safety line and a tentative smile. Her knees felt a little wobbly when the scaffold lifted off, but she was fine as long as she didn't look down. At least that's what she kept telling herself.

Chance stood right beside her, a reassuring arm around her shoulders and the safety line around his waist. He'd gotten some strange looks from his crew when he buckled up, but a deal was a deal.

"What do you think?" he asked after they stepped off the scaffold and onto the platform.

Having conquered her initial fear, she could answer honestly, "It's beautiful!"

Even the wind held its breath at the dramatic blend of brilliant sky and rolling terrain.

Grass tall enough to hide a man on horseback covered the far hills, shimmering silvery-green in the sunshine. Closer to home, dark red windrows striped the fallow fields. Her healthy tomato plants looked tiny, but she could definitely make them out on the west side of the farmyard, while the weathered house and outbuildings stood as monuments to the pioneers who'd erected them.

Chance didn't feel his usual restlessness as he surveyed the land that had been in Joni's family for four generations. Quite the opposite, in fact. And wasn't that odd? He'd always had a wanderlust that couldn't be quenched. But there he stood, at the top of the world, fighting the urge to put down roots and make some plans for the future.

Joni turned to him, her safety line stretching taut and her smile as trusting as a child's. "I feel so free—like I've grown wings!"

He studied her sun-kissed cheeks, tinged pink now with excitement, and the eyes as big and blue as the sky behind her. And though it pained him to admit it, he knew it would never work. Simply put, oil and water didn't mix.

Taking her by the elbow, he guided her back on board the scaffold. "We'd better be going."

"But we just got here." She didn't understand his abrupt about-face.

He gave Skinny the signal to bring them down, and the rumble of the diesel engine precluded a reply.

They rode to the rig floor in silence, with him trying to put her out of his mind and her trying to figure out what thoughts churned behind his forbidding scowl.

Not until her feet touched solid ground did it occur to Joni that she'd been too preoccupied to feel any fear on the way down. Two small steps in the right direction, she realized proudly.

Chance knew why she was smiling and wanted to congratulate her. Instead, he kept his voice impersonal. "I'll send one of the guys over to the trailer to help you load up."

Her voice held a faint reediness. "Will you be coming home for supper?"

"No."

"Oh."

The silence stretched as taut as a drilling cable about to snap.

She toyed with her wedding ring, turning it back and forth on her finger. "Any sign of oil yet?"

In danger of touching her, he shoved his hands, palms out, into his rear pockets. "There was a show in the sand, but we'll have to bore deeper."

"Did you send a sample to the state."

"Yes."

"Have you gotten the results back yet?"

"They called me this morning."

She saw something flicker over his face before he masked it. "What did they say?"

"What difference does it make?" A muscle jumped along that Mount Rushmore of a jaw. "If I didn't think there was oil here, I sure as hell wouldn't be wasting my time drilling for it."

Joni remembered his caustic remark about his grandfather's hat and realized that the geology report from the state hadn't been good. Disappointment swamped her, not so much for herself as for Chance.

When had the man become more important than the money? Maybe from the first moment she'd laid eyes on him. Lord knew, he'd had her going in circles ever since.

She opened her mouth to tell him that she really didn't care about the oil, that she'd rather have him than all the crude in Oklahoma, when the mud pump throbbed and drilling got under way again.

"I'd better get back to work," Chance said, and turned to climb the steps that led to the rig floor.

"What time will you be home tonight?" Joni knew she sounded like a clinging vine, but she couldn't help herself.

Halfway up the steps he stopped and turned back, casting a long shadow over her. "I think it's best for both of us if I just live in the trailer from now on.

She clomped up after him until she stood nose to chest with him. "What about the Fourth of July parade?"

"What about it?"

"You promised Grandpa he could ride in your convertible."

"That was before—" He broke off in mid-sentence and made a taut, thin line of his lips to seal the unsavory words inside.

Her body strained toward his. She loved

the smell of his skin—the scent of honest labor mixed with his healthy man odor. "Before what?"

"Forget it."

"Before what?"

Chance didn't want to hurt her, but she'd left him no choice. "Before I realized that I can't hang on to anything and you can't let go of anything."

Joni recoiled as if he'd struck her, then rallied on the strength of her love. "You hung on to your grandfather's hat."

"A stupid sentimental gesture on my part." He rebuffed her attempt to read any significance into it.

She grabbed handfuls of his T-shirt. "Why is it so damned difficult for you to admit you care?"

"I don't know what the hell you're talking about." He clutched her wrists so hard they hurt.

She held on as tenaciously as a bulldog, grinding her knuckles into the solid wall of his chest. "Does it make you any less a man to admit that you kept the hat because you loved your grandfather?"

"No more than it makes you any less of a woman to admit that you had no control over Larry's actions."

"What do you mean by that?"

"I mean I know that Larry killed himself."

Shock made her grip go slack. "Who told you?"

He forced her hands down. "I also know that you found him in the barn when you got home from work, and—"

"Who told you?" she repeated tautly.

He ignored this inquiry too. "That you're still blaming yourself because you weren't there to stop him."

"Dr. Rayburn talks too much for his own good." She remembered the men standing out in the driveway the night of the dance and put two and two together.

"And you talk too little for yours," he said harshly.

She wrenched her wrists free of his bruising hold. "What right do you have to go snooping around behind my back, anyway?"

"You took me for twenty thousand dol—"

"I did no such thing!"

"You knew I wanted to drill where—"

"I was desperate!"

"You couldn't collect on Larry's life ins—"

"I had nowhere to go, no one to turn to."

"Your loan application was rej—"

"I thought you were the answer to our prayers."

He nailed her in place with a hard stare. "You're getting pretty good at leading me around by the nose, aren't you?"

She turned the full blue blaze of her eyes on him. "I don't deserve that!"

"A kiss here, a feel there." He made it sound so calculated on her part, she felt sick. "If it weren't for Grandpa, I'd have to wonder who drew the map."

She looked at him, stunned. That he could think her capable of such a terrible betrayal after all she'd been through... Somehow, the past and the present became tangled in her mind. And something inside of her snapped.

"Damn you, Larry Fletcher!" Joni swung blindly, the stinging crack of her palm hitting a chiseled cheek. She was striking back the only way she knew how. "If you weren't already dead, I'd kill you myself!"

But it was Chance who wore the dark red imprint of her deep-pent rage. Chance who raised his hand in retaliation, then dropped it. Worse yet, it was Chance who left her standing on the steps in a welter of guilt and confusion, calling over his shoulder from the rig floor, "Go home, Joni, before I hurt you worse than Larry did."

Sad to say, he already had.

Chapter 8

The Fourth of July dawned as faultless and clear as a perfect diamond.

Joni spent the better part of the morning packing a basket for the picnic supper that would follow the parade and precede the fireworks display. She fried chicken just the way Grandpa liked it, with lots of crispy brown crust, then deviled a dozen eggs and iced an angel food cake for dessert.

That done, she went outside and picked some ripe red tomatoes to slice and chill. With the bread and butter sandwiches she'd already made, they would round out the meal.

She felt a boundless sense of accomplishment as she checked the rest of her beautiful tomatoes. Next spring, she planned to expand her acreage and branch out into other vegetable crops. The food broker she was dealing with in Oklahoma City had told her there was a growing market for specialty produce. Asparagus, beets, baby carrots, broccoli, spinach...The possibilities were endless.

It might not be farming as Grandpa had known it, but small-scale intensive operations like this could improve farm income and diversify the economic base in rural areas. Better yet, it might well be the way to keep the homestead in the family.

The steady rhythm of the drill reminded her of the more immediate problem. Chance had neither called nor come by the house since the day she'd slapped him, and she could only assume that he wasn't going to the parade. That left her to drive the pickup, which suited her fine, but Grandpa had really been looking forward to riding in the convertible.

In all honesty, Joni wasn't sorry she'd slapped Chance. Not that she believed physical violence ever solved anything, but he'd asked for it with that insulting remark about the map. What she regretted more than anything was that Grandpa had to suffer as a result of her actions.

As she reached to pluck another tomato, a clang of the dinner bell drifted from the porch. One ring meant that Grandpa needed to talk to her, but it wasn't an emergency. Anymore than that meant that he was having trouble breathing and she should run like a cat with her tail on fire. They'd devised this system because his voice wasn't strong enough to carry over the noise from the rig, and so far, it had worked real well.

She waved to signal she'd heard the bell, then headed back to the house.

"Chance just called." Grandpa looked as happy as a heifer in the corncrib, which was a welcome change from the hangdog expression he'd been wearing all week.

"What did he want?" Joni tried to keep her voice on an even keel, but a note of excitement jiggled it nonetheless.

"He wanted to know what time the parade started."

She grabbed hold of the porch railing for support. "And?"

"When I told him three o'clock, he said he'd pick us up at two."

Her heart did handstands, knowing he hadn't left them in the lurch. She linked her arm through Grandpa's and, laughing, led him toward the screen door. "What are we standing around here jawing for? Time's a-wasting."

Joni fed Grandpa a light dinner, then helped him into the tub in the downstairs bathroom and scrubbed him up one side and down the other. He decided to take a short nap before he put on his suit, which left her free to shower and shampoo and get dressed.

They were ready and waiting when Chance turned into the driveway a few minutes before two. He looked so handsome in creased jeans, a mint-green polo shirt with the collar unbuttoned, and that gorgeous raw silk jacket, Joni's stomach pulled all sorts of crazy shenanigans when she opened the screen door for him.

"Hi," she said shyly, wishing she had something a bit more eloquent in the way of a greeting.

"Hi," he returned, his mobile mouth splitting into a smile as he surveyed her outfit with obvious relish.

Joni had taken Grandpa at his word and raided the cedar chest in the attic again. Her grandmother's dress, a drop-waisted delicacy of ivory chiffon and intricate lacework, had required only the mandatory tucks in the bodice to fit as if it were made for her. With it she wore matching stockings as sheer as a spider's web and a pair of low-heeled pumps she'd bought on sale several years back.

But it was what she wasn't wearing that most intrigued Chance.

She wasn't wearing her wedding ring on her left hand anymore.

His glance flicked from her bare left hand to her right, where the plain gold band now claimed its proper place. Then his eyes sought hers and he wanted to drown in the fathomless depths of her.

"You've come a long way, baby," he quipped, but his expression told her he wanted to take her the rest of the way.

"I'm taking it a step at a time," she whispered, and her expression begged him not to rush her.

But time was their enemy, flying by on Mercury's wings without regard for their hearts' wishes.

As if they needed a reminder, the long-case clock in the entryway chimed out the musical prelude to the hour, and then the hour itself. One...two.

"If we don't get moving pretty soon," Grandpa prodded as he tottered out of the living room in his shiny blue serge suit and old straw boater, "I'm going to be sneezing dust."

Chance got Grandpa settled in the Thunderbird and put their picnic basket in the trunk while Joni ran to get the poster-board-sized signs she planned to display during the parade.

"I was going to tape them to the doors of my pickup," she explained when Chance asked to see the signs. "But now that we're going to ride in the convertible, Grandpa and I can just hold them in the air."

Chance thought he came a little closer to understanding what made Joni tick when he read what she'd printed in red and blue Magic Marker on the white posterboard.

The first sign declared: AS LONG AS WE HAVE ONE SEED LEFT, WE'LL PLANT.

And the second proclaimed: AS LONG AS WE HAVE ONE OUNCE OF STRENGTH, WE'LL PLOW.

"Those are old sayings around here," she told him, never dreaming he'd find them as meaningful as she did.

"Well, I can think of a lot better use for your arms than wearing them out waving signs." His expression was altogether too sexy for her not to know what he was talking about. "Go get the masking tape so we can show them off properly."

"But the finish on your car—"

"The tape marks will rub off."

She loved him so much, she ached with it. "I'll be right back."

They taped one sign to the passenger door and one to the driver's, then got into the convertible.

Chance told Grandpa to hang on to his hat and away they went.

Grandpa had been elected grand marshal by the parade committee because he was the oldest and best loved resident of Redemption County, so Chance steered the Thunderbird into line directly ahead of the mayor's long black Lincoln and right behind the high school band.

The majorette raised her baton. The band struck up an off-key rendition of "Yankee Doodle Boy." And the parade started down a Main Street straight out of a Norman Rockwell painting. All across America people celebrated the nation's birthday. Veterans marched with flags and heads held high. Backyard chefs in funny hats and burlap aprons fired up their grills. Umpires shouted "Play ball!" and families converged for their annual reunions. But nowhere in the Land of the Free did the patriotic fever burn brighter than it did in Redemption.

Sure, farmers were hurting. In addition to the always capricious weather, they were faced with specific problems, including their own overproductivity. A surplus of food had caused prices to fall. Shrinking foreign markets, tumbling land values, and increasing debt had fueled bankruptcies and foreclosures galore.

But farmers fought, bought, and thought American. And one day a year they showed the world that they believed they lived in the greatest country on God's green earth.

The way Grandpa waved his boater, a body would have thought he was running for governor. Nobody waved back because everybody was in the parade. That didn't bother him. He just waved to the people behind him.

No sooner had the high school band gotten the hang of George M. Cohan's classic song than the parade turned in to the city park and began dispersing. Several participants stopped by to congratulate Grandpa on a job well done, and more than a few of them commented favorably on Joni's signs.

Chance parked the convertible in the shade of a big old cottonwood tree and got Grandpa situated at a picnic table while Joni took their basket from the trunk.

She flagged Dr. Rayburn down and invited him to join them when supper was served. His wife had died a couple of winters ago and he depended on the largess of his patients at occasions like these.

"Are you sure you've got enough to go around?" Mustache fluttering, the physician eyed her cake carrier with what could only be termed a gluttonous gleam.

"I'm sure," she said.

"You know how Joni is," Grandpa added as an incentive. "She always cooks enough to feed Coxey's Army."

Dr. Rayburn hooked his thumbs in the bright red suspenders that held up his rumpled white pants. "In that case, I'd be pleased to join you."

Supper was scheduled for six o'clock, which left almost two hours for fun and games.

But first, the formalities.

The band played "The Star-Spangled Banner," making up with heart what they lacked in harmony. Everybody stood and everybody sang.

Then the mayor made his usual long-winded speech. And as usual, nobody listened.

Finally, the potato sacks came out, and the ropes for the three-legged races, and the horseshoes appeared for pitching.

The hot sun had the picnickers begging for their next breath.

Chance shrugged out of his jacket and went in search of something cold to wet his whistle. Joni saw Loretta West sitting by herself on a blanket on the ground and wandered over that way.

"Two small steps in the right direction," Loretta said when she noticed that Joni had moved her wedding ring.

"Three," Joni corrected her friend, and went on to describe her scaffold ride, skipping the details of her fight with Chance.

"You went up against your fear and it worked."

"Surprised the heck out of me too."

Loretta looked at Chance, who stood head and shoulders above the other men gathered around the beer keg. "He's been good for you in ways that Larry never was."

Joni turned a puzzled glance on her friend. "How so?"

"Understand, I don't mean to speak ill of the dead."

"I understand."

The blonde pursed her heavily glossed lips, as if trying to think how to phrase it. "Larry took the sparkle out of your eyes and the smile off your lips long before he died."

"I felt so guilty because I couldn't make him happy." Joni plucked a blade of grass and split it in two with a smooth oval thumbnail that had profited from regular exposure to an emery board. "I still feel guilty sometimes."

"But some people are just born unhappy." The cut-out arms and straight, tight skirt of

Loretta's red leather body skimmer set off her curves to full advantage. Now she tucked her legs under her and settled into a more comfortable position. "It's part of their genetic makeup or something."

"It's an interesting thought, I'll grant you that."

Loretta nodded in the direction of the picnic table. "Look at your grandfather."

A smile curved Joni's lips when she saw Grandpa stacking the deck against Dr. Rayburn, who'd joined him for a game of pitch. "He's really something, isn't he?"

"If anybody ever had good reason to put a gun to his head, it was him."

"I remember him saying once that he'd been dusted, busted, but never rusted."

"Why do you think he's one way and Larry was the other?"

"The difference in their personalities, I suppose."

Loretta smiled her butter-almond smile. "I rest my case."

She then gave her spindrift hair a proud pat. "Who says all blondes are airheads?"

The two women looked at each other and burst out laughing. When their mirth subsided, they whiled away the afternoon talking about this and that.

Loretta had a new boyfriend, but she wasn't naming names. "I've had such bad luck in my relationships, I'm afraid I'll jinx it if I say too much."

"He's single, I presume?" Joni remembered the supposedly divorced truck driver whose wife and three children had shown up on Loretta's doorstep one revealing spring day. As it had turned out, Loretta was just one of several girlfriends along the guy's route.

"For sure," Loretta said fervently. "One thing I learned from that last jerk is that a man who'll cheat with me will probably cheat on me."

Joni played Twenty Questions, trying to guess the identity of the man who'd captured the perennial bridesmaid's interest, but she didn't know any more about him when the supper call came over the loudspeaker than she had when she'd started.

"Keep me posted," Joni said as she stood and turned toward her picnic table.

"You'll be the first to hear," Loretta promised.

Joni lifted their platter of fried chicken from the basket and almost dropped it when Chance came up behind her and began nuzzling her neck right there in front of God and Grandpa.

She set it down and spun around, only to find herself trapped between the concrete table and his long, equally hard body. "Have you been drinking, for heaven's sake?"

"No, ma'am." He handed her his paper cup and she took a tentative sip.

"Lemonade!" she exclaimed, surprised.

"Yes'm." His smile packed a hundred-proof wallop all its own. "I want to be in full control of my faculties tonight."

The minister asked everyone to bow their heads just then, and Joni was only too happy to comply. She squeezed her eyes shut and prayed for guidance, but she knew that something that felt this right couldn't be wrong.

"Amen," the picnickers said together, then sat down at their individual tables and dug in.

"Pass the tomatoes," Dr. Rayburn requested when he had some of everything else piled on his plate.

Grandpa pointed a well-gnawed chicken leg at Chance. "You know the only two things that money can't buy?"

Chance smiled, expecting a joke. "Can't say as I do."

Grandpa glanced at Joni, then back at Chance, as if silently bestowing his blessing on them. "True love and homegrown tomatoes."

The lemonade in Joni's cup sloshed perilously close to the rim as she lifted it to her lips.

"Haven't heard that one in a blue moon," Dr. Rayburn said as he reached for another bread and butter sandwich.

Chance noticed that Joni had been doing more sipping than supping. He placed a deviled egg on her plate, his eyes making promises galore, and said matter-of-factly, "Gotta keep your strength up."

Joni looked down at the paprika-sprinkled egg all alone on her plate and smiled. She knew exactly what he meant. "Pass the chicken, please."

But if she thought he was going to leave her to eat in peace, she had another think coming. His leg touching hers under the table, their thighs brushing when he leaned forward to reach for the salt shaker, his fingers skimming along her sensitive palm when he handed it to her—by the time she finished supper, even the fine hairs on her arms were attuned to his covertly erotic signals.

Exhaustion and excitement finally caught up with Grandpa. Dr. Rayburn offered to run him home and help him into bed, and by way of thanks, Joni gave him the rest of the angel food cake.

"Grandpa seemed stronger today then he has since I've been here," Chance remarked when they were gone.

"Don't expect it to last." Joni's voice quavered as she explained that Dr. Rayburn had recently warned her that Grandpa's old heart couldn't withstand too many more of those terrible coughing spells.

Chance drew her into his arms, hurting for her, and buried his face in her cascading hair. "Cry if it'll help, little darlin'."

Joni laid her cheek in the warm hollow of his wide shoulder, but the tears she badly needed to shed just wouldn't come.

They stood for a long time in the cricket-stitched silence, just holding each other.

"I owe you an apology," she finally whispered against his muscular chest.

"For what?" He sounded perplexed.

"For what I said when I slapped you."

"But not for slapping me?"

"No." She raised her head and met his mildly amused eyes. "You deserved that."

"I guess I did," he admitted with a rueful smile. Twilight lay like a gray velvet mantle over the park as they broke apart and began clearing the table.

Joni packed up their basket and Chance put it back in the trunk of the Thunderbird.

Then he took out the soft blue blanket he'd brought, spread it under the lacy branches of the cottonwood, and drew her down with him.

The fireworks weren't scheduled to start until full dark, and everyone seemed to have the same idea as Chance.

Mothers sat and rocked fussy babies. Fathers called the older children back to the family fold. Young couples necked in dusk's accommodating shadow.

"Didn't you want children when you were married?" Chance smiled when a rebellious little boy reached over and pulled the pigtails of the cute little girl on the next blanket. Damned if it didn't remind him of something he'd have done at that age.

"We discussed it." Joni made out a man's shape on Loretta's blanket. He looked familiar to her, but she couldn't see his face in the deepening twilight. Silently she wished her friend good luck in her new relationship.

"But?" he prompted softly, sliding his hand up her slender back and under her rich red hair.

"We never got beyond the talking stage." And she wouldn't have felt right about bringing an innocent baby into their foundering marriage.

"*Never?*" he asked teasingly, trying to lighten the maudlin moment he'd unwittingly promoted.

The answering tinkle of her laughter told him that he'd succeeded. "You know what I mean."

Someone produced a fiddle then, someone else a guitar, and soon the strains of "Old George Gans" made time roll by. The music arose in Scotland, followed its migrant people across ocean and mountain, and finally settled in Redemption, Oklahoma.

Everyone raised their voices in song for "Bluetail Fly" and "Frère Jacques," then one of the picnickers requested "Red River Valley."

From this valley they say you are going.
We will miss your bright eyes and your smile...

Chance kept one hand lightly on the back of Joni's neck as he sang along. Ripples skipped up her skin as she joined in, her husky contralto in perfect accord with his clear, resonant baritone.

Come and sit by my side if you love me,
Do not hasten to bid me adieu;

But remember the Red River Valley,
And the girl that has loved you so true.

Seesawing between sensation and sad-ness, Joni looked at Chance. Butterscotch drops of moon drizzled down through the cottonwood branches, the golden light glancing off his high-planed cheekbones. She could smell his evergreen soap and see the wanting in his eyes. And she realized she couldn't let him leave Redemption with-out showing him how much she loved him.

"Let's go home." Were they her words or his? It didn't matter, for two minds had the same thought.

Silently they stood and folded the blan-ket, their fingertips grazing as they brought the corners together. Arm in arm they walked to the Thunderbird, their pulses setting the pace.

He circled her shoulders with his right arm and studied her upturned face, his con-science speaking louder than his body now. "You understand I have to leave when I'm finished with the well?"

Joni swallowed the lump in her throat, knowing that trying to tie him down would be like trying to tether the wind. "When will that be?"

If she backed out on him now, he'd never forgive himself for opening his big mouth. He had to answer her honestly, though. "A couple of days, a week at the most."

But her heart had already made up her mind. "Then let's make good use of the time that's left to us."

Chapter 9

Grandpa was sawing 'em off on the sofa sleeper, Sooner at his side, when Joni and Chance got home.

The bluetick hound raised its black nose in greeting when they tiptoed into the dining room, then snugged it back between its paws when they left on equally silent feet.

Chance turned off the porch light, Joni the hall light, and then there was only moonlight streaming through those sparkling windows and the dark at the top of the stairs.

Nervous now, she wiped damp palms on her chiffon skirt and tried to think of something to say. Something clever like, "My room or yours?" But her throat and mouth felt so cottony, the words wouldn't come.

He realized this was a big step for her and wanted to help her along. Scooping her into his arms, his widow with the warrior's heart, he said softly, "Let's go upstairs."

She wrapped her arms around his neck, only too happy to let him take charge, and breathed into the dark rain cloud of his hair, "I'm sorry—it's been a while."

"For me too," he admitted throatily, the thought of finally having her naked beneath him making him feel a little dizzy as he lithely climbed the stairs.

Joni raised her head and searched those eyes of incandescent green, almost electric in their intensity. Dare she ask? She jumped in with both feet. "How long?"

"Does it really matter?"

"Yes and no."

Chance remembered the women he'd known before, the ones who'd demanded nothing of him. Not even honesty. But the woman in his arms now deserved more. "There's been no one else since I met you."

She bit her lip, relief mingling with a vague regret for those who'd gone before her. "It's been three years for me."

He hated himself for being glad she hadn't given herself to anyone since her husband, but was glad nonetheless. "Sounds like we've both got some catching up to do."

Not wanting any ghosts coming between them tonight, he bypassed her room in favor of his. She thrilled to his flexing muscles as he let her feet slide slowly to the floor. From the beginning she'd felt his fire. Now she wanted to feed the flame.

He crushed her to him, molding her legs,

her hips, her breasts to the fevered length of his body. From the first he'd made her for a scrapper. Now he wanted to make her burn.

Neither heard the tick of the bedside clock as their mouths met. And neither thought of the calendar hanging in the kitchen when their tongues mated. Time lost all meaning as their deliciously heated kiss deepened into an act of love.

His fingers located the buttons at the back of her spun-sugar dress and, one by pearly one, undid them. Despite four years of marriage, being undressed by a man was a new experience for her. But as she slid her hands up the silky lapels and under the broad shoulders of his jacket, she found that two could play this exciting game.

No matter what they were doing with the rest of their bodies, they were determined to stay joined at the mouth.

It made for some funny gymnastics and laughter bubbled between their lips when Joni couldn't get his polo shirt off without breaking the connection.

Then he reached to switch on the bedside lamp and she made a grab for his hand. "Please—leave it off."

Chance's breathing was ragged. "I want to see you."

"I'm not very...big." Joni's voice was as thin as vapor.

"More than a handful's a waste." He cupped her bare breasts in his callused palms, finding her all the woman he'd ever want.

And later, when the light did come on, the volcanic pleasure in his eyes touched her in a way his hands could not.

Her doubts dissolved, her hands indulged in their own orgy of discovery. No amount of imagining could have prepared her for the feel of him.

She found him sinuous and tough, scarred and lean. His neck and shoulders were as smooth as polished bronze, yet alive and supple. The hair on his chest—so crisp and curly—softened the sharp edges of his pectoral muscles. She loved the way it swirled around his flat nipples, then made a racing stripe down his springboard of a stomach before fanning out again at the base of his...

He grabbed her curious hand. "Didn't you ever hear about what happens to girls who play with fire?"

She smiled and squeezed. "They get burned."

Chance groaned and drove closer. "Then burn, baby, burn."

Joni did just that, stoking his ardor with

bold caresses that brought her endearments spiced with expletives and, at the point of conflagration, his restraining hand.

"Not yet," he murmured.

A heat she'd never experienced before started deep in her belly and spread quickly out to her limbs when he lowered her to the bed and dropped beside her in a full-length embrace. She watched his gaze wander over her nakedness, the fervor in his eyes firing her skin.

His fingers, callused from the miles of drilling cable he'd handled yet sensitive to a woman's needs, flickered from her dusty-rose nipples, down the delicate bow of her ribs, to the moist cleft between her thighs. His tongue followed—a living flame—and she melted from the inside out.

Chance moved up over her, sliding into her with an ease that surprised her. Joni opened her eyes to find him watching her while his hips thrust in slow, rhythmic strokes.

"I wish you'd been the first," she whispered.

He wished it, too, but smiled down without showing it. "As long as I'm the last."

She touched his lips and took the plunge. "I love you, Chance."

"I love you too, Joni." He found a freedom in saying it that he'd never dreamed possible.

Their mouths met in another ardent kiss and their bodies kept time to the distant drum of the drill bit. Their hearts echoed its primal beat.

Gradually, his strokes increased in tempo. Eventually, she spun out of control. And finally, they whirled in a fiery pas de deux to a loving climax.

Much later they lay entwined in the tangled sheets, basking in an afterglow that would have shamed an aurora. A lover's moon nestled up to the window. Stars winked from on high. The night-perfumed air fanned their damp bodies, and they fell asleep in each other's arms.

~ ~ ~

Chance woke to the creak of a floorboard.

In that first fuzzy moment of arousal, he thought he must have dreamed it. Then he straightened his head around on the pillow and saw her, clothed only in moonlight, bending down to pick up her dress. He knew then this was no dream.

"Joni?"

She picked up her slip.

He braced up on his elbows and glanced at the digital clock. Two-thirty. "I know you're a compulsive cleaner, but this is ridiculous."

She picked up her shoes.

When she started toward the door, still without a word of explanation, he levered himself off the bed and went after her. She had nightmares. Maybe she walked in her sleep as well.

"Come on, Joni." He gripped her upper arm gently so as not to disturb her. "Back to—"

"Let go of me, Chance." Her low, strangled warning shot his sleepwalking theory all to hell.

He stared down at her bowed head, her wildfire hair, and tightened his fingers on her tender flesh. "Not until you tell me what you're doing."

"I'm going back to my room."

"Why?"

"You were right about me all along, Chance." She raised her head, and it was then he saw the glistening tracks of tears on her cheeks. "I can't let go."

Swearing softly, he released her arm and took her in both of his, feeling her pain as if it were his own. "Joni, Joni, please don't cry."

A small sob escaped her. "I thought I could go through it again—the loving, the losing—but I can't."

He felt a shudder possess her body and pinched his eyes shut. "I'll be back in a month, six weeks at the most."

"And then you'll leave again."

"It's how I make my living."

She broke free of his embrace, beyond reason. "And what am I supposed to do while you're running footloose and fancy free all over the state of Oklahoma?"

Anger stirred the coals of a more compelling emotion. "If you're so damned worried about what I'm going to be doing while I'm gone, then why don't you marry me before I go?"

"*Marry* you?"

"Yeah, marry me."

She poked his firm shoulder with a furious finger. "What kind of proposal is that?"

He raked an aggravated hand through his hair. "The kind a man makes when he and the woman he loves are buck-naked and butting heads in the middle of the night."

They stood so close that Chance's shadow blocked the moonlight from her upturned face. But he could feel her rapid-fire breathing hitting his bare chest, and he knew that it was just a matter of time until she recovered from the shock.

For her part, Joni wasn't sure she'd ever

have the power of speech again. She loved him, no two ways about it. And she'd be lying through her teeth if she said she'd never entertained the fantasy of marrying him. But she'd already had a glimpse of the future, and she couldn't stand any more good-byes.

She said as much. "I'm not interested in being a part-time wife. Nor do I like the idea of kissing my husband hello one day and good-bye the next."

"The telephone and bookwork I do now from the trailer I can do from here," he argued. "So I'd be home a lot more than you think."

"Half the time, at best."

"Then take the best."

She opened the door and started across the hall, shaking her head. "I love you, Chance, but I just can't see myself in a hit-and-miss marriage."

"Be reasonable, Joni." He followed her into her room, feeling as if he were fighting for his life. In a very real way, he was. "I wouldn't enjoy the good-byes any more than you, but it would make for some pretty damned exciting hellos."

She switched on her bedside lamp, not the least bit embarrassed by her nudity. Quite a coup, for her. "What if something came up and I needed you here?"

He trailed her to her closet, wondering if he'd ever get enough of her. "I'd never be more than a day's drive from home."

"A lot can happen in a day."

"I'll buy an airplane."

She put her shoes on the shelf, then reached for a hanger for her dress. "Is this the same man talking who gave me all that trouble about the twenty thousand doll—"

"What the hell is that?" Chance interrupted coldly.

Joni turned around in time to see a gust of fury pass across his face. Confused, she asked, "What?"

He pointed an accusing finger at the clothes in her closet. "That."

She looked back at Larry's jeans and shirts still hanging beside her skirts and dresses and felt her knees buckle. They'd been there so long—

"And all this time I thought it was Larry who was haunting you." His rusty tone of voice sounded like a death knell in the silent room.

She turned tormented eyes to him. "I completely forgot they were—"

"The truth is, you won't let him rest in peace."

Auburn hair flew every which way as she

shook her head in frantic denial. "That's not—"

"You've even got a different hair shirt for every day of the week."

"Grandpa kept Grandma's—"

"In a cedar chest in the attic, not in his bedroom closet."

"Please, Chance, let me ex—"

"Actions speak louder than words, Joni."

She held out her hands, pleading for understanding. "I used to lie awake at night, blaming myself and wondering what I'd done to make him so—"

He spun on his heel and strode across the room.

"I love you," she beseeched his broad, retreating back.

In the doorway he paused and looked over his shoulder with something like pain in his eyes. "The price of loving is letting go."

~ ~ ~

Things went from bad to worse when Joni dragged herself out of bed at just after daybreak and found that Grandpa's feet were so swollen, he couldn't get his shoes on.

"Are his hands and face puffy too?" Dr. Rayburn asked when she called him at home.

"Yes, but remember, he ate a lot of salt on his tomatoes yesterday." With the receiver braced in the hollow of her shoulder, Joni stood before the kitchen counter, fixing Grandpa's breakfast.

"How's his breathing?"

"He sounded like a suction pump when I came downstairs."

"Did you give him his medicine?"

"First thing this morning." She buttered Grandpa's toast and cut it in half, remembering with a twinge of regret how Chance had reacted when she'd challenged him about having beer for breakfast. Come to think of it, he never did drink it.

"I'll swing by the house on my way to the office," Dr. Rayburn said before they hung up. "But in the meantime, keep him in bed."

Grandpa wasn't very talkative when Joni first carried his breakfast tray into the dining room. She knew he didn't feel well. But when he even failed to inquire as to Chance's whereabouts, she knew that he must have heard the muffled slap of the screen door in the middle of the night. The fact that Chance hadn't slammed the door behind him but had closed it quietly made his departure seem that much more final. Loud noises were second nature to Joni. She could shout and stamp and slam with the best of them. But silence...

Silence was a killer.

Larry had been the silent type. When she'd married him, she'd considered it a sign of strength.

Only now, three years after she'd buried him, was she beginning to see that it could also be a fatal character flaw.

He'd never been one to discuss his feelings. Even during their courtship and the early years of their marriage she'd had to be content with the rare "I love you." But as their debts had mounted, he'd grown more and more distant. He'd skipped meals, claiming he wasn't really hungry. He'd sit alone in the living room, staring at the wall. When she'd called his name to rouse him, he'd stumbled upstairs to bed and turned his back to her.

Joni had begged him to talk to her, to see a counselor, but misplaced masculine pride had tied his tongue. He hadn't seemed to understand that the shame wasn't in having a problem, but in not doing anything to solve it. Even Grandpa, who'd never meddled in their marriage, had felt compelled to put his two cents' worth in. He'd tried to tell Larry that their farm deficits weren't all his fault, but Larry had turned a deaf ear.

Then came that fateful day when the mortgage company had delivered the foreclosure notice. Larry had gone to the mailbox—later, she'd followed a trail of discarded letters and bills from their rural mailbox at the side of the road to the barn. She couldn't presume to know what had gone through his mind when he'd found it, but he probably hadn't stopped to think about that exclusion clause in his life insurance policy. Already depressed, he'd probably seen it as the final straw.

She'd blamed herself for being at work. And who wouldn't have after coming home and discovering her husband dead in the barn, a bullet in his head and a gun in his hand? Who wouldn't have played judge and jury with her own soul? Found herself guilty of crimes of the heart? Crimes that only now was she learning she hadn't committed.

And she'd been mad. Damn good and mad, though she hadn't even realized until she met Chance how much anger she harbored. If Larry had ever really loved her, how could he have pulled the rug out from under her like that?

There were no easy answers to her questions. No convenient outlets for her rage. Joni realized that Chance was right. The price of love was letting go of the anger and the guilt. Only when she'd purged herself of those destructive emotions could she quit clinging to the past and begin embracing the future.

Grandpa spooned up a bite of soft-boiled egg, his spirits improving now that his medicine was taking effect. "Who were you talking to on the phone?"

"Dr. Rayburn." She reached to adjust the shutter above his bed, letting in a buttery-yellow stream of sunshine. "He's going to stop by in a little while."

"I wonder if he'll have time for a game of pitch." Grandpa's breathing sounded better, but he still looked puffy.

She pulled up a chair and sat down beside the sleeper sofa. "Don't you ever give up?"

"Would I be drilling an oil well at my age if I did?" The wrinkles that threescore years and ten had etched into his face deepened in a smile.

Joni could see the men climbing on the rig from the dining room window, but from this distance she couldn't tell if any of them was Chance. "I suppose not."

"Yessireebob..." Grandpa dunked a corner of his toast into his coffee. "You sure can tell a lot about a man by the way he loses at cards."

She gave him her I'm-on-to-you-mister look.

He chewed the soggy toast, then swallowed it and wiped his whiskery chin. "A good loser, he'll just smile and challenge you to another hand."

Joni remembered Chance laughing and referring to Grandpa as "Diamond Jim Brady," then rolling up his sleeves and going back for more.

"But a sore loser..." Grandpa took a sip of his coffee. "He'll walk away mad and probably take it out on someone else."

Now she remembered Larry coming to bed one night shortly after she'd married him, blaming her because Grandpa had pulled a fast one on him and refusing to play anymore.

"I'd rather play with a good loser because he's more fun." Grandpa set his cup in the saucer with a shaky hand, then cleared his throat. "By the same token, I'd rather beat a sore loser because he's got it coming."

"More eating and less talking, if you please." She knew he meant well, but it didn't make her feel any better. It only made her sick to realize how much time and energy she'd wasted feeling responsible for Larry's taking the coward's way out when, in reality, he'd chosen to go that route.

Grandpa ate another bite of egg, then set his spoon down with an apologetic smile. "I'm really not very hungry, darlin'."

Joni kissed the top of his grizzled head, then picked up the tray. "You rest till Dr. Rayburn gets here."

She scraped his leftovers into the dog's dish and straightened up the kitchen, but she did everything automatically. Her mind was back in her bedroom with Chance. She was still arguing with him over his marriage proposal, still experiencing that painfully revealing moment when he'd found Larry's clothes hanging in her closet.

As long as she was coming to grips with the truth, she asked herself how she would have felt if the shoe had been on the other foot. If, for instance, he'd demanded that she give up her farm and go with him. Or worse yet, if she'd discovered another woman's belongings in *his* bedroom.

The pounding of the drill bit drew Joni out onto the porch. She turned remorseful eyes toward the rig, seeking but not finding Chance, remembering the bleak expression in his eyes just before he'd left her last night. He'd offered her the best of himself—the laughter and the loving, his support in moments of crisis and his memory in times of absence—and she'd given him nothing but grief in return.

Wasn't Chance McCoy half the time better than Chance McCoy none of the time? Could he find it in his heart to forgive her for behaving as selfishly in her way as Larry had in his?

Those questions and others rode the red wind across the porch. Something in the air stung her nostrils, burned her eyes, but she was too busy planning her next move to pay much attention to the discomfort.

When Dr. Rayburn got here, she'd go over to the drilling site and lay her cards on the table. She'd tell Chance that she loved him enough to let him go, that she'd be waiting here to welcome him—

A diabolical tremor suddenly shook the earth and a sinister hiss from the rig drowned out all other sounds, even the rhythmic hammering of the drill bit.

Joni looked in that direction, her stunned expression hardening to horror when she saw the derrick rocking back and forth...back and forth...like a huge erector set about to topple.

Not again! she screamed silently, watching the roughnecks leaping willy-nilly off the swaying rig and thinking that if anything happened to Chance, they'd have to open another grave for her.

The bottom dropped out of her stomach when she didn't see Chance's muscular figure among the men running for cover. Without regard for her own safety, she dashed down the porch steps and raced pell-mell toward the cornfield.

In the excitement she hadn't heard Grandpa start coughing in the dining room. Nor did she notice Dr. Rayburn's car now coming to a stop in the driveway. All her energies were concentrated on getting to Chance.

"Blowout!" someone shouted over a growling rumble and the hissing of a thousand snakes.

"Beat it!" Someone else waved her back as the ground around the rig humped like an angry cat.

"Please God," she prayed over and over again, her nose and throat and lungs burning with every breath of the noxious air. "Don't let him die."

Her prayers were answered when she collided with six feet of solid muscle at the edge of the site.

Chance, moving full speed in her direction, knocked her backward to the hot, heaving earth and slammed his weight, hard and warm, atop her.

Joni, landing spread-eagle, wrapped her arms around his neck and wreathed his lean thighs with her legs just as all hell broke loose.

A roar of a hundred cannon ruptured the air. The ground trembled at the shock of the blast. Sand and mud burst from the hole; casing pipe shot out as straight as it went in.

Chance hugged the ground like a man under shell fire, crushing the breath from her lungs. Joni clung to him for dear love, smothering her screams against his chest. Rocks and flying debris flailed the backs of her hands, as if trying to break her grip. He held her fast, absorbing her terror, until the blowout spent itself with a final shudder and a rude spew of...

Sulfur water.

Neither of them even noticed they hadn't struck oil. They had eyes only for each other.

"You little idiot!" Chance levered up and screamed down at her. "What'd you mean by running to the site like that? You scared me half to death."

"I thought..." Joni traced the chiseled planes of his face with trembling hands, whispering prayers of thanks that came straight from the heart.

"Didn't you *see* me waving you back?"

She nodded, touching his eyes, his nose, his mouth with feather-light fingertips.

"You could've been killed, for God's sake!"

"So could..."

His fierce green eyes still mirrored the elemental fury of the moments they'd shared and survived. She lay beneath him, her heart windmilling from the force of it and her love for him. Their combined body heat seemed to fuse them together.

"Joni..."

"Chance..."

Roughnecks rushed back to the rig.

His mouth ground down on hers. She answered him with a hungry little moan. His tongue speared between her lips; hers welcomed him home.

The odor of sulfur singed the air.

Salt mingled in their kiss and sweat heightened the male smell of him, so musky and alive that she forgot everything—even the gravel grinding into her back.

A dinner bell clanging frantically in the distance finally broke them apart. Dr. Rayburn stood on the porch, ringing it for all he was worth.

"Grandpa!" Joni knew immediately that something was wrong.

Chance jumped to his feet, then hauled her up and clasped her hand tightly in his. "Let's go!"

Neither one of them ever remembered the particulars of their frenzied journey, which probably took all of two minutes. Their breaths beat fast and stitches knifed their sides. She stumbled once in the middle of the cornfield. His strong arms kept her from falling. But in their minds, it forever remained a blur of wind and fear.

Dr. Rayburn opened the screen door for them.

"Grandpa?" Joni shook so badly that Chance could feel his own body being jerked by hers.

The physician's shoulders drooped like his mustache as he ushered them into the dining room. "He's dying, Joni."

"If you want to take him to the hospital, I'll drive," Chance offered, wanting to do everything in his power to help.

Joni bowed her head, battling the temptation to break her promise, but keeping it in the end. "He wants to die at home."

Grandpa lay on the sleeper sofa, his eyes closed. He looked to be at peace, though his lungs fought valiantly against the enemy's grasp.

Scalding tears blurred Joni's vision as she sank to her knees and covered his knobby old hands with her own. "Grandpa?"

"Joni?" His eyelids flew open, but he appeared to have difficulty focusing on her. "Where's Chance?"

"Right here." Chance crouched beside Joni, his reassuring hands forming the final link in a chain of love.

"Did we...strike oil?" Grandpa's voice was so faint, they had to lean closer to catch the words.

Chance weighed the evil of lying against the greater good of easing the old man's passing. No contest there. "We hit a gusher."

His bloodless lips curved in a smile; his eyelids drifted closed. "A gushhh..."

Joni gave a strangled cry when she felt his hands go limp beneath hers and realized he'd just left his emotional and physical pain behind him forever.

She wanted to call him back; instead, she placed her lips to his incognizant ear and let him go gently. "I love you, Grandpa."

Chance tried to say something, but found his throat too clogged for words. He looked at Grandpa, whose strength of spirit lived on in the woman he loved, and bid a silent good-bye to one hell of a man.

They remained bedside, heads bowed and hands joined, while Dr. Rayburn notified the funeral home by telephone. When the attendants arrived, Chance helped Joni lay out Grandpa's blue serge suit, clean white shirt, and striped necktie.

Word spread like wildfire in the close-knit county. People came in droves all day long, bearing casserole dishes and condolences. By nightfall the kitchen bore a strong resemblance to an emergency relief center.

Apple cake and peach cobbler shared counter space with carrot pudding and blueberry pie. Platters of barbecued brisket, sugar-cured ham, and crispy fried chicken covered the table. A pot of fresh green beans flavored with bacon bubbled on the stove.

Even after the roughnecks had eaten their fill, there was food to spare.

Joni pressed a platterful on Dr. Rayburn, who'd left before the onslaught and come back after completing his hospital rounds. "If you run out, there's more where that came from."

"This ought to do me for a while," the physician said with a sad smile for the circumstances that had prompted his windfall.

Chance saw him to the door, then returned to the kitchen to find that Joni had disappeared. Some sixth sense guided him into the dining room.

She stood beside the sleeper sofa, staring down at Sooner. The bluetick hound raised soulful eyes to the two human faces, but refused to budge from its master's bed.

"Dogs grieve too," she whispered brokenly, and in that instant her three-year drought came to an end.

Joni cried for her grandparents, reunited at long last. She cried for her parents, whom she barely remembered. And she even cried for Larry, who'd betrayed her trust.

Chance picked her up and carried her into the living room. Then he lowered himself into the overstuffed club chair and comforted her. And when she was all cried out, he carried her upstairs to his bedroom and made love to a woman who was finally free of her past.

Chapter 10

Softly and tenderly Jesus is calling. Calling
for you and for me...

Redemption County turned out in full
voice to reunite Bat Dillon with his beloved
Ruthann. The mourners clustered about the
family and the flower-bedecked casket sang
their hearts out. No one needed a hymnal, for
these were words long committed to memory.

Come home. Come home.

Ye who are weary, come home.

Grandpa, as almost everyone but Dr.
Rayburn had called him, was free now of the
pain and the sorrow that had pockmarked
his long and very productive life, but he'd
left behind a legacy that nothing could mar.

Chance stood at Joni's side on that rolling
green hill in the Redemption cemetery, his
hand at her elbow and his heart in his eyes.
He'd put Tex in charge of plugging the well
and shutting down the site. It occurred to
him now that the trustworthy roughneck was
long overdue for a promotion to supervisor.
Not only would it reward a good employee for
a job well done, but it would give Chance

more time to spend with Joni—an important consideration for a man who was making honeymoon plans for the end of next month.

"Let us pray," the minister intoned when the final notes of Grandpa's favorite old hymn had been swallowed by the wind.

Joni brushed her auburn hair back off her face and bowed her head. She felt Chance put his arm around her waist and leaned closer to him, giving silent thanks for his constant presence since the blowout.

She'd been wearing her hair loose night and day, as much to symbolize her own personal victory over the past as to please the man who'd freed her from it. But she knew she'd yet to pass the true test of her new-found love—the letting go—so she sent a couple of extra prayers winging heaven-ward, asking for the courage she'd need when the time came.

"Amen," the minister said, bringing the simple graveside service to a conclusion.

Even though the mourners would be gathering at the farmhouse shortly, they filed past Joni and Chance, offering private words of condolence before going to their cars.

Dr. Rayburn was first in line, and Joni couldn't thank him enough for all he'd done for Grandpa.

"Bat was lucky to have you," the physician said.

"No luckier than I was to have him when my parents were killed," she pointed out.

Dr. Rayburn shook hands with Chance then. "He sure thought the world of you."

"The feeling was mutual."

"Give me a call when you get back. We'll play some cards and pitch some bull."

Chance nodded. "Will do."

Tex and Skinny and the other roughnecks were next. They wore their Sunday best, which was quite a departure from their everyday clothes. Each one of them had put his share of quarters in Grandpa's pocket. And as they walked away smiling, Joni realized that each one of them was a good loser.

Neighboring farmers, the mayor, even Jesse James—dressed in banker's gray, of course—had a funny story to tell, a favorite memory to relate.

Finally, Loretta West and Simp Creed stepped up to pay their respects. Joni couldn't get over the change in her friend's appearance. Loretta wore a conservative black dress that perfectly complimented Simp's "early undertaker" suit, and her normally tousled platinum hair was pinned back in a sleek chignon. Even her makeup had been toned down, though her eyelashes were as long and lacy as ever.

The men made small talk; the women played catch-up.

'When did this come about?"

"Ladies' choice at the crossroads."

Joni snapped her fingers, remembering then. "That's who was sitting on your blanket at the Fourth of July picnic."

Loretta's eyes shone like the prairie moon as she displayed her quarter-carat engagement ring.

Joni and Chance remained behind as the newly engaged couple started down the hill. They wanted to make their final goodbye together. And they wanted to make it alone.

The wind whipped the streamers on the wreaths piled high around Grandpa's casket. Joni plucked a red rose from the arrangement, draping it to place in the cedar chest, while Chance sprinkled the red dirt he'd brought from the drilling site over the top of it. The simple ceremony completed, they stood a moment in silent remembrance.

Chance drew her into his arms then and bent his head low over hers. "He loved you so much."

"He loved you too." Joni heaved a sob and

buried her face in his starched white shirt-front.

Rocking her back and forth, his voice and hands replete with tenderness, Chance felt the loss as deeply as Joni did. And if he shed a tear or two himself...well, it was something that was long overdue.

"Better?" he asked softly when she raised her head.

Sniffing, she nodded.

"Let's go home."

"I have one more stop to make."

Chance searched her tear-streaked face, stared gravely into her eyes. "Do you want me to go with you?"

Joni looked up entreatingly and shook her head. "I have to do this alone."

The relentless wind plastered her black skirt to those endless legs as she crossed to Larry's headstone. Kneeling in the sweet-scented grass, she removed the plain gold band from the third finger of her right hand and set it at the base of the stone. It was time for her to let him rest in peace. And as she stood and turned her back on the guilt and the anger, she knew it was past time she got on with her life.

Arms linked, Joni and Chance started down the gentle green hill. They hadn't found black gold. But thanks to his grandfather and hers, they'd found something far more precious than the oil they were originally seeking. They'd found love.

~ ~ ~

Two cans of sweetened condensed milk, two tablespoons of vanilla, one quart of whole milk, one pint of half-and-half, and one pint of whipping cream—

"What're you doing?"

"Making ice cream."

Chance lazed back against the kitchen counter and let his eyes have free rein with those long, freckled legs and that scantily clad bottom. He should have left a week ago, but he kept finding excuses to stay. "I thought you had to cook it first."

"Not this recipe." Joni stirred the rich mixture with a wooden spoon until it was thoroughly blended, then poured it into the four-quart freezer can. That done, she set the whole kit and caboodle in the refrigerator to chill before churning.

"Wouldn't it be a lot easier to just go buy a gallon of ice cream at the grocery store?" He wondered what she was wearing under her pink flowered short shorts. The bikini panties that barely covered her titian curls or the French-cut teddy that sent his pulse into overdrive?

"Easier, yes." She rinsed her hands at the sink and dried them on a towel, then got a metal hammer from the tool drawer and a glass measuring cup out of the cupboard. "Better, no."

Bikini panties and no bra, he decided when she turned around to face him. Raising both hands, he lightly raked the backs of his fingers over her small, firm breasts. Her nipples hardened against the soft cloth of her fuzzy pink tank top, and he felt a corresponding stiffness in his jeans.

Joni almost lost her grasp on the utensils she was holding as lightning splintered along her nerve endings, striking deep at the molten core of her. Day or night, it never failed. All he had to do was touch her and her control went flying out the window.

"Here," she said, breaking the charged atmosphere by handing him the hammer before she dropped it. "Make yourself useful as well as distracting." Turning then, she led him toward the back door.

Chance kept his eyes on her trim bottom as he followed her from the kitchen to the enclosed back porch. Funny, how his taste in women had changed. He used to prefer candy-box curves. But recent and frequent experience had convinced him that the meat was always sweetest close to the bone.

His blood came to a full boil when she raised the lid on the chest-style freezer that stood against the west wall and leaned down to get something out of it. "How long does that stuff in the refrigerator have to chill?"

She came up with a bulging cloth bag and an impish grin. "About as long as it'll take you to chip fifteen pounds of ice."

He pulled a grudge of a face. "That wasn't exactly what I had in mind."

She wrinkled her nose in mock disapproval. "If you want to eat ice cream, you have to help make it. House rules."

"I've worked up an appetite," he grumbled good-naturedly, reaching for the heavy bag she held, "but not for ice cream."

Joni laughed and measured out three cups of rock salt to mix with the ice he was crushing. This last week had been the happiest of her life—packed with more laughter and more loving than she'd ever dreamed possible. Just as sure as the world's turning, though, their time together was drawing to an end.

Speaking of which..."Tex called while you were outside working on the tin lizzie."

"What'd he want?" He halted in mid-action, his expressive green eyes locking with her anxious blue ones. They both knew that the old car was just an excuse—and a flimsy one at that—for him to hang around the house a little while longer.

Keeping her voice casual, she carried the rock salt into the kitchen. "He said the core samples at the new site look great, and that he's ready to raise the rig whenever you are."

"I'll call him when I'm finished with this." Chance gave the ice a vicious *whack* with the hammer, crushing a good five pounds with one blow. He'd never been torn between a woman and his work before. But then, he'd never been in love before either.

She set the full cup on the counter and, alone, pressed her fingers to her lips as if that might help her control the urge to beg him not to leave her. When she felt properly composed, she drifted back to the doorway and began stockpiling another memory to sustain her in his absence.

Naked to the waist, he wielded the hammer with strength and surety. Afternoon sunshine poured through the jalousied windows and sweat sheened his copper skin, running down the muscles that rippled with each lithe movement of his chest and arms.

She never tired of looking at him—at the angle of his jaw, the line of his eyebrow, the crisp black thickness of his hair. More than anything, she wanted to be with him on a full-time basis—to sleep with him every night and to wake up with him every morning. For now, though, that was an impossible dream.

"All done," he announced, setting the hammer aside and smiling at her from across the porch.

"I'll make the ice cream while you make your phone call." She turned away before she burst into tears.

Forty-five minutes later the ice cream had been packed for hardening and Joni sat on Chance's lap, facing him and helping him lick the dasher clean. Her thighs were draped over his and she held a dinner plate between them to catch the melting drops they missed.

When the dasher was all licked up, they set it and the plate on the table. Then she looped her arms around his neck and he linked his hands at the small of her back.

"You're smeared from ear to ear," he murmured, touching his tongue to the corner of her sticky mouth.

"So're you." Laughing now, she returned the favor, the taste of him making her feel as woozy as those sips of wildcat whiskey she used to sneak as a teenager.

"Uh-oh." His lips were cold, his breath warm, as he bathed her face like a mother cat washes her kitten. "I missed a couple of spots."

"Those are freckles," she protested softly, her body pulsing in places she wished he'd cool when he turned his attention to the sensitive, speckled column of her throat.

Neither one of them had mentioned his impending departure yet, partly because their tongues were already occupied and partly because talking about it would have spoiled the playful mood.

Eventually, though, she had to ask and he had to answer.

Joni ensnared his hair in her fingers and lifted his head. "When are you leaving?"

Chance slid his strong hands up her slender thighs and under the legs of her shorts. "Sunday morning."

So little time...

"Will you miss me?" She gave a start, then grew lax and soft when his adroit thumbs slipped inside her bikini panties.

He discovered to his great delight that she was already wet for him. "Would the heavens miss the stars?"

They kissed, sharing their vanilla essence with unselfish ardor. His mouth captured her moans while his tongue and thumbs circled gently. She dropped her hands to his broad shoulders, clung crazily as he took her through peaks and valleys and left her panting for more.

"How long will it take the ice cream to get hard?" he asked when they broke apart.

"A couple of hours," she whispered breathlessly. "Why?"

He stood with her a-straddle his waist, her legs locked behind him, and carried her out of the kitchen. "'Cause it's going to take me at least that long to get soft."

~ ~ ~

"Tired?" he asked at the bottom of the stairs.

"Kind of," she admitted at the top.

It had been a busy day, what with Chance helping Joni pick tomatoes and Joni helping Chance pack for tomorrow's trip. After supper they'd cleaned up and gone out to the crossroads so he could make his good-byes. They'd danced once, a slow dance, and then come straight home to spend the rest of the night alone.

"*Too* tired?" Considerately, he put his heart's desire on hold as he paused to open the door to the bedroom they now claimed as their own.

"Never." Casting a look of invitation over her shoulder, she preceded him into the relatively austere room that was in such stark contrast to her old lace-and-wicker retreat.

Moonlight filtered in through simply curtained windows and reflected off polished wood and white plaster, magnifying the feeling of space and suspending all sense of the world beyond.

Furnishings, while minimal, were made of bird's-eye maple and had a history all their own. The mirrored dresser had come from Scotland with Joni's great-grandparents, the chest of drawers had been her grandfather's wedding present to her grandmother, and the nightstands her father's gift to her mother.

A delicately colored checkerboard quilt covered the antique brass bed that four generations of her family had been conceived in. Joni hoped to continue the tradition with Chance.

"Whew!" His smile now would have charmed the stripe off a skunk. Not to mention the clothes off a redhead. "You had me scared for a minute."

"What's the matter, tough guy?" After folding back the quilt, she left her blue jersey dress and half-slip, her bra and bikini panties in a heap on the floor. Then, wearing nothing but her freckles and a puckish grin, she spread her arms out to her sides and fell backward onto the bed. "Afraid you'll have to go without a proper good-bye?"

By way of answer, he dropped his shirt and jeans and shorts in a haphazard trail from the door to the bed and laid down on top of her. Wedging her knees apart with his, he settled his body between her receptive legs and kissed her long and hard.

"If that's good-bye," she said throatily when he raised his lips from hers, "I can hardly wait for hello."

His hand stroked up the inside of her thigh and his dexterous fingers found her dewy with anticipation. "You know what they say about all good things coming to those who wait."

They kissed again, taking time to savor every bit of each other before impatience claimed them for the first of many farewells that night.

"I love you, Joni," he whispered as he sheathed himself in her satiny warmth, making her body a part of his and his a part of hers.

"I love you too, Chance," she murmured as she palmed his firm buttocks and drew him in so deep, he could feel her heart beating.

The wind swished the curtain on the sill.

He sank his fingers into her red, red hair and spread it across his pillow. "I still get the shakes when I remember you running onto the drilling site the day of the blowout."

She gently bit the meaty muscle of his bicep, thrilling to the taste and the texture of his living flesh. "I thought you were going to die and I wanted to die with you."

"If you ever do anything like that again, I'll..." He lowered his head and nipped her neck in loving punishment.

"You'll what?" she challenged him softly. Now he let his tongue make reparation. She threaded her fingers through his thick hair and pulled on it until he raised his head. "You'll what?"

"I'll..." He made a grinding motion with his hips that robbed her of breath. "That's what."

She smiled and answered with a movement of her own. "Remind me to have my running shoes resoled."

They kissed then, handing themselves heart and soul into the other's keeping.

"I want to see us..." Chance levered up and hung his head to watch their bodies mingling.

Joni's eager eyes followed.

Moonlight cast a mellow glow on the place where dark met fair, where male met female, illuminating the physical evidence of a spiritual bond that neither time nor distance could ever dissolve.

He reared his head back then, his eyes and his body boring into hers with all the passion and power a woman could want.

Joni had lived in Redemption her whole life, while Chance had been a roamer for as long as he could remember. Together now, they came home.

~ ~ ~

"Joni?"

"In here."

Chance paused in the kitchen doorway, his mind entertaining several provocative ways to say goodbye, when she turned away from the counter and he saw that she was wearing one of his old white dress shirts. The sleeves had been rolled back to her elbows, and the hem struck her mid-thigh, accenting those freckled legs that went on forever.

Joni curled her bare toes on the morning-cool linoleum but stood perfectly still otherwise as his electric-green eyes traveled from the shadowy triangle at the top of her thighs to the magnificent halo of hair that framed her pensive face.

"You're not making this any easier," he chided her quietly.

"Good," she said fiercely.

He studied her, standing there in his shirt and her own stubbornness, and decided this was going to be his last trip for a while. A *long* while.

She looked at him, dressed to leave her in clean jeans and bleached white T-shirt, and wished he'd give her something tangible to hold on to until he came back.

"I'm finished packing the car," he said, his eyes never wavering from her sweet-sad face.

"Did you find that people bag I made?" she asked, her mouth trembling mutinously.

He nodded. "I put it in the cooler."

She glanced at the clock over the stove, trying not to dote on the hard-muscled sight of him filling her doorway. "I guess this is good-bye then, huh?"

"No."

"No?" Her startled gaze returned to his

face, and what she saw there made her run-away pulse throb at her throat.

He crossed the kitchen in two purposeful strides and pulled her to him, nearly lifting her off the floor. She wore nothing beneath the shirt, having shed her inhibitions about her body in his arms, and the rough denim of his jeans rubbed enticingly against her legs. Then his mouth came down on hers, hot and hungry, and she melted into his kiss.

"*That's* good-bye," he whispered gruffly when he raised his head.

Her fingers wanted to linger in his dark hair, but she forced them down. "Good-bye, Chance."

Taking her hands in his, he turned them over and pressed his lips to the center of one and then the other of her now healed palms. "Promise you'll wear your work gloves while I'm gone."

Nodding, she raised her eyes to his and extracted a promise of her own. "Swear you'll wear your safety line when you go up on the platform."

It seemed to take as much effort on his part to release her as it did on hers to let him go.

Morning sunshine streamed in through the multipaned windows, and the kitchen seemed laden with the sounds and the smells of home. The cuckoo clock ticked the minutes off. Fresh coffee perked on the range. Sooner whimpered where he lay curled in the corner, probably chasing rabbits in his sleep.

Chance took a couple of steps backward, realized he was dragging his feet, and spun on his heel.

Joni followed him to the screen door, her greedy eyes drinking in black hair and bronzed skin, her sealed lips damming a flood of frantic entreaties.

The clock in the entryway chimed eight times.

She trailed him out onto the porch. The old oak swing creaked in the wind and her aching heart cried, *Please don't go!*

At the top of the steps he turned to her and said. "Wait there. I'll be right back." Chance bounded down the steps and across the driveway, where the Fiesta Red Thunderbird convertible waited to whisk him away.

Her spirits dipped to a new low when he cut around to the driver's side. But instead of opening the door and getting in, as she'd feared, he reached over it and grabbed something off the seat.

The tears she'd promised herself she wouldn't shed trickled heedlessly down her cheeks when he came to the bottom of the porch steps and tossed his grandfather's hat up to her.

She caught that ribbonless old relic and hugged it to her heart.

"I'll be back in a month," he said. "Six weeks at the most."

Her forget-me-not eyes shone expectantly. "I'll be waiting."

Epilogue

She heard it before she saw it barreling round the bend, the roar of its engine riding the country air like an eagle aboard a thermal. It was rare that any vehicle appeared on this remote stretch of highway. Rarer still that that vehicle would be a restored '56 Thunderbird.

Top down and chrome flashing almost painfully in the hot August sun, the classic Fiesta Red convertible rocketed by pastures and cows and trees as though the devil were tailgating it.

"You're the Reason God Made Oklahoma" blasted at full volume from the radio, adding to the already fervent pitch of wind and speed.

The driver had his right hand on the steering wheel, his left arm crooked on the convertible's door, and his mind on a woman with million-dollar legs.

Joni stripped off her work gloves when she realized who it was and went tearing down the driveway to meet him. Gravel flew from beneath her feet and her red hair streamed behind her like a banner in the wind. She had so much to tell him, was so eager to get her hands on him, she couldn't wait for him to come to her.

She'd made good use of her six weeks alone.

The food broker in Oklahoma City has been so impressed by the quantity and the quality of her tomato crop that he'd signed her up on the spot to plant some broccoli for a fall harvest. She was growing it organically, of course—no insecticides unless absolutely necessary. Better yet, the extra cash meant she could afford to have the house painted before her wedding day.

She'd decided she wanted to get married at home. Dr. Rayburn had agreed to give her away, and while rearranging things in the attic, she'd run across her grandmother's wedding dress. A romantic delicacy of silk embroidered chiffon, it hadn't needed a single alteration. Now she was thinking in terms of turning her old room into a nursery.

Chance had some news himself.

He'd promoted Tex to supervisor and hired another geologist to take the core samples and analyze them. He'd still be putting the deals together and making the final decision on whether or not to drill. But he could do more of his work from home now and less from the site.

Not only that, but he'd bought Joni's wedding gift while he was gone. It was a rocking chair made of bird's-eye maple, the perfect finishing touch for the bedroom he planned to share with her for the rest of his life. The antiques dealer had sworn on a stack of Bibles that he'd ship it to Redemption in time for their wedding day.

Chance slowed the Thunderbird and turned into the entrance to the farm. Then he stopped and reached across the seat to open the door. "Going my way, pretty lady?"

"Always and forever." Joni didn't have to be asked twice. She jumped into the car and slid over to sit hip to hip beside him, then gave him a kiss that put his pulse in fast forward.

With the wind at their backs then, the widow and the wildcatter went home.

ALSO AVAILABLE IN LARGE PRINT

THE LADY AND THE CHAMP by Fran Baker

ISBN: 0-7862-5216-2

"A warm, wonderful knockout of a book"
Julie Garwood, *New York Times* bestselling author

SAN ANTONIO ROSE by Fran Baker

ISBN: 0-7862-3915-8

"As fresh and beautiful as the rose for which it is named"
Romantic Times

KING OF THE MOUNTAIN by Fran Baker

ISBN: 0-7862-3910-7

"Beautifully written! Don't miss this one."
Rendezvous

Ask for these titles at your favorite bookstore or local library

About the Author

Fran Baker is the bestselling author of ten books and hundreds of articles, book reviews, author interviews and opinion pieces. Readers are invited to contact her via her web site at www.FranBaker.com.

We hope you have enjoyed this Large Print book. Other Delphi Books titles are available at your library, through your favorite bookstore, or directly from us via our website or by calling (800) 431-1579.

For information about titles, please visit our Web site at:

www.DelphiBooks.us

To share your comments, please write:

Delphi Books
P.O. Box 6435
Lee's Summit, MO 64064

Printed in the United States
25529LVS00002B/1-66